Strangeville School
Is Definitely Not Cursed

illustrated by
BRETT HELQUIST

STRANGEVILLE SCHOOL
IS DEFINITELY NOT CURSED

by
DARCY MILLER

RANDOM HOUSE 🏠 NEW YORK

Text copyright © 2022 by Darcy Miller
Jacket art and interior illustrations copyright © 2022 by Brett Helquist

All rights reserved. Published in the United States by Random House Children's Books, a division of Penguin Random House LLC, New York.

Random House and the colophon are registered trademarks of Penguin Random House LLC.

Visit us on the Web! rhcbooks.com

Educators and librarians, for a variety of teaching tools, visit us at RHTeachersLibrarians.com

Library of Congress Cataloging-in-Publication Data
Names: Miller, Darcy, author. | Helquist, Brett, illustrator.
Title: Strangeville School is definitely not cursed / by Darcy Miller; illustrated by Brett Helquist.
Description: First edition. | New York: Random House, [2022] | Series: Strangeville School; 2 | Audience: Ages 8–12. | Summary: When a glowing lost-and-found box appears and stranger-than-normal things begin to happen at Strangeville School, it is up to Harvey and his friends to solve the mystery of a fifty-year-old curse before it is too late.
Identifiers: LCCN 2022010945 (print) | LCCN 2022010946 (ebook) | ISBN 978-0-593-30993-3 (trade) | ISBN 978-0-593-30994-0 (lib. bdg.) | ISBN 978-0-593-30995-7 (ebook)
Subjects: CYAC: Middle schools—Fiction. | Schools—Fiction. | Monsters—Fiction. | Blessing and cursing—Fiction. | Horror stories. | Humorous stories. | LCGFT: Horror fiction. | Humorous fiction. | Novels.
Classification: LCC PZ7.1.M565 Sr 2022 (print) | LCC PZ7.1.M565 (ebook) | DDC [Fic]—dc23

The artist used oil on paper to create the illustrations for this book.
The text of this book is set in 11.65-point New Century Schoolbook LT Pro.
Interior design by Jen Valero

Printed in the United States of America
10 9 8 7 6 5 4 3 2 1
First Edition

For Fitz and Wyle —DM

Contents

Strangeville School
Is Definitely Not Cursed

1

Welcome Back

Good morning, Strangeville students, and welcome back! I hope you've all had a *wonderful* weekend!

This is Vice Principal Capozzi speaking, filling in for Principal Gupta, who, three days into our game of hide-and-seek, has still yet to be found. Well done, Principal Gupta, although you can't hide forever! Sooner or later, the wolves will sniff you out. . . .

Well, I hope you all remembered to wax your nostrils and shine your earlobes this morning, because it's picture day at Strangeville School! I'd like to remind all students that blinking while being photographed is *strictly* forbidden. Any student caught blinking *will* receive a mark on their permanent record.

And not the *good* kind of mark, either . . .

In other news, the French club is holding their annual bake sale in the East Hallway this morning, so make sure to stop by and say "bonjour!" Lots of tasty treats will be available for purchase, including fresh croissants, chocolate éclairs, and homemade blood sausage!

Mmm, mmm. Blood sausage!

Moving on, it looks like the wart on my left foot has finally gone away!

And, finally, I'm excited to announce that our beloved lost-and-found box has, once more, mysteriously appeared in the cafeteria! Make sure to stop by before it vanishes into thin air yet again!

No need to worry about the strange, eerie glow coming from the lost-and-found box's depths; I'm sure it's all perfectly fine!

Nurse Porter has already recovered several missing bone saws from the box, and just this morning I found a pair of socks I've been missing since 1987! There are quite a few more holes in them than I remember, and the left toe is full of spiders, but still. What an exciting discovery!

That's all for now, Strangeville. Have a great day!

I know the spiders will. . . .

Show-and-Smell

In Mr. Sandringham's first-period classroom, Stella Cho leaned forward in her seat, poking Harvey Hill in the back with a pencil.

"Ow!" Harvey said, turning around to look at her. "Did you just poke me in the back with a pencil?"

"Of course not," Stella said innocently, slipping the pencil back into her sleeve. Stella was short for her age, with long black hair, 371 eyelashes, and a highly developed sense of curiosity. As lead reporter for the *Strangeville School Gazette,* she always had several writing utensils stashed about her person, just in case.

Harvey narrowed his eyes suspiciously at her.

He was tall for his age, with wavy brown hair, 372 eyelashes, and a highly developed sense of caution. As lead photographer for the *Strangeville School Gazette,* he was never without the old-fashioned camera hanging from a strap around his neck.

Oh, and he also had wings.

Yes, wings.

(What, have you not read the first book?)

"We should check out the lost-and-found box after homeroom," Stella told Harvey. "Get some pictures for the newspaper."

"I don't know," Harvey said, tugging at his ear. "It sounds a little . . . weird. I mean, why is it *glowing*? And what's the deal with it just *appearing* out of nowhere?"

Stella shrugged. "It's just a box," she said. "What could possibly go wrong?"

Harvey, who could think of at *least* sixteen things off the top of his head that could go wrong, opened his mouth to reply. But before he could speak, their homeroom teacher clapped his hands for attention.

"Eyes up here, please," Mr. Sandringham said. "We have just enough time for a quick round of show-and-smell before the bell rings. Evie, I believe it was your turn next?"

Evie Anderson stood up and joined Mr. Sandringham at the front of the classroom.

"Hey, everyone," she said, giving the class a wave. "So, for show-and-smell today, I *was* going to bring one of my brother's dirty socks, but my dad did laundry last night. So instead I brought *this,* which I found in the back of our refrigerator."

Reaching into her pocket, she unwrapped a crinkled piece of tinfoil to reveal a gooey, greenish-yellow lump of . . . *something.*

The smell was not good.

In fact, it was awful.

In fact, it was unbelievably, *inconceivably* terrible.

It knocked Harvey back in his seat, his eyes watering and his stomach heaving and his nose burning from the terrible stench.

"It smells like death," Arjun Narula observed, pulling his T-shirt up to cover his nose.

"Yes, doesn't it?" Mr. Sandringham asked in a strangled voice, coughing into the crook of his elbow. "How wonderful. Would anyone like to guess what it is that Evie brought today?"

Twenty-two hands shot up in the air.

"Rotten sardines?"

"Curdled cottage cheese?"

"Expired coleslaw?"

"Rancid baked beans?"

"Ooh, ooh, I've got it!" Nicolas Flarsky said, bouncing up and down in his seat. "Is it a piece of Stinking Bishop cheese?"

Stinking Bishop, as everyone knows, is a soft, washed-rind cheese made from the milk of rare Gloucester cattle, matured in humid, cavelike conditions and sold primarily in the United Kingdom.

It is not unusual for there to be spots of mold on the leatherlike rind of Stinking Bishop, which is considered a delicacy by cheese enthusiasts worldwide. The cheese itself is an oozing, luscious paste with a surprisingly subtle, nutty flavor.

But, anyway.

Enough about Stinking Bishop!

Let's get back to Harvey.

He was turning slightly green around the edges.

"Actually, I'm not really sure *what* it is," Evie admitted to the class. "But there's one way to find out!"

As the rest of the students watched in fascinated horror, Evie popped the lump of greenish-yellow *something* into her mouth and began chewing thoughtfully.

After a moment, a strange look crossed her face.

Reaching up, she spit the *something* back into her hand and held it up for the class to see.

"Well," Evie said. "It looks like I found one of my brother's socks after all."

The
Lost-and-Found Box

Harvey was right: the lost-and-found box was *definitely* weird.

For one thing, there was the way it looked. Harvey had been expecting a cardboard box—square, or maybe even rectangular—with the words LOST AND FOUND scribbled across the side in Sharpie.

Instead the lost-and-found box was an elaborately carved wooden chest, nearly three feet long and almost as tall. It looked old, the wood weathered with age and the sides strapped with thick iron bands.

There was also a strange, greenish light spilling

from the top of the open chest: an eerie, otherworldly glow that seemed to somehow shimmer and pulse with a life of its own. Looking at it made Harvey feel cold and hot and sleepy and *wide awake,* all at once.

It also made his left armpit itch, for some reason.

"Cool," Stella said, waving her hand over the lost-and-found. Her fingers turned green as she swished them back and forth in the strange, greenish light.

Harvey took a step back.

"Um, this thing looks really old," he said nervously. "Are we sure it isn't radioactive?"

"Lots of things are radioactive," Stella told him, crouching down to poke through the open chest. "Smoke detectors, magazines, kitty litter . . . even bananas!"

"Oh," Harvey said faintly. "That's . . . comforting."

He took another step back from the chest.

Stella sifted methodically through the lost-and-found's contents, poking through the jumble of discarded mittens and abandoned toys, misplaced sunglasses and winter hats.

Harvey scratched his armpit. "What are you looking for?" he asked, pushing himself up on his tiptoes to see over Stella's head.

"I left half a peanut-butter-and-baloney sandwich in my desk last week," Stella said. "But this morning it was gone. I thought someone might have turned it in."

Harvey blinked. "Did you say peanut butter and *baloney?*"

"Of course," Stella said, glancing over her shoulder. "Why?"

Harvey opened his mouth, and then shut it. "Never mind," he said.

"Anyway," Stella said with a little sigh, "it doesn't look like it's here. Can you grab a few pictures of the box before we go?" she asked. "The bell's going to ring soon."

Harvey swallowed.

Reluctantly he edged his way nearer to the lost-and-found.

Up close, the chest's strange greenish light made his *right* armpit itch as well.

He raised his camera and took several shots of the lost-and-found box from different angles. The wooden box seemed to hum with a life of its own, drawing Harvey closer and closer.

Now that he thought about it, the eerie green light coming from the box was actually sort of . . . *beautiful.*

In fact, it was *so* beautiful that it was impossible to look away.

But why would Harvey *want* to look away?

The box was fantastic.

It was amazing.

It was *mesmerizing.*

It was— Wait a minute.

At the very bottom of the chest, he caught a glimpse of something shiny.

Without realizing quite what he was doing, Harvey knelt down and lifted the *something* from the bottom of the box.

It was a compass.

The battered brass case, its surface dented with age, fit perfectly in Harvey's hand.

It reminded Harvey of the compass his grandfather, a famous adventure photographer for *National Geographic* magazine, had once owned. Before his death, Harvey's grandfather had traveled the

world, scaling the highest mountain peaks and crossing the harshest deserts to capture the perfect shot.

Harvey had always wanted to follow in his footsteps one day.

Even though he didn't particularly like heights.

Or heat.

Or sand.

Or, really, when he thought about it, *adventure* in general . . .

The compass caught the light, glinting dully in his hand. A warm glow washed over Harvey in response, enveloping him completely.

For a moment, everything felt . . . *right*.

It was almost as if the compass was *meant* for him.

Was it a sign?

Was it an omen?

Was it *fate*?

"What are you doing?" Stella called from the doorway, interrupting Harvey's trance. "Come on, we're going to be late for gym!"

Harvey swallowed, his fingers tightening around the compass.

"But don't we have music class next?" he asked Stella, stalling for time. He *knew* that taking the compass was wrong.

But still . . .

Was anyone really going to *miss* it?

"That was *last* week," Stella told Harvey. "*This* week we have gym next." She paused, shaking her head. "I can't believe your old school had the same schedule all year long. Talk about *boring*."

Harvey wasn't really listening.

After all, who *knew* how long the compass had been sitting at the bottom of the box, just gathering dust?

Wasn't it better for someone to *use* it?

Harvey knew he was making excuses.

Maybe it was the way the compass fit perfectly in his hand.

Maybe it was the way it reminded him of his grandfather.

Maybe he just liked shiny things!

Whatever the reason, Harvey couldn't help himself.

He slipped the brass compass carefully into his pocket.

"Coming," he called to Stella, stumbling to his feet. As he left the cafeteria, he turned to give the lost-and-found box a final, uneasy glance.

Then, his armpits still itching, he followed Stella into the hall.

The Curse

"*Discipline!*" Coach Johnson thundered, planting her fists against her sides and peering around the gymnasium. "Today you puny pustules will finally learn the meaning of the word! Today you will exhaust yourselves, both mentally and physically! You will push yourselves further than you ever thought possible! You will leave *everything* on the court!"

Harvey leaned over to Stella in alarm. "I thought we were playing Wiffle ball today."

Stella gave Harvey a strange look. "We *are* playing Wiffle ball," she said. "Why, how did you play it at your last school?"

Harvey swallowed hard.

He had been at Strangeville for less than a month and was still getting used to his new school.

"Never mind," he said, leaning back. He could feel the compass he'd taken from the lost-and-found box shifting in his pocket as he moved.

Harvey froze.

What if the compass fell out? What if someone recognized it? What if they *knew* what Harvey had done?

The thought made the tips of his ears grow red and his palms dampen with sweat.

Harvey had never stolen anything before.

He was beginning to suspect that he wasn't cut out for a life of crime.

"*Discipline!*" Coach Johnson barked again, making Harvey jump. "You will learn it; you will live it; you will *love* it! When it comes to gym class, and when it comes to life, *discipline* is the only thing that separates us from the animals!"

Stella raised her hand. "I thought opposable thumbs were what separated us from the animals."

"Wait, I thought monkeys had opposable thumbs too," Nicolas said, turning to look at Stella.

"Most *primates* have opposable thumbs," Nevaeh

corrected him knowledgeably. "Some monkeys have *pseudo*-opposable thumbs."

Nevaeh was a tall, serious-looking girl who wore her hair in side puffs and flossed after every meal. In honor of school picture day, she was dressed in spotless white.

"Am I the only one who doesn't know what 'opposable' means?" Evie asked.

"It means you can do *this*," Arjun said, pinching his fingers and thumb together and pretending to grasp something. "I saw a show on Animal Planet about it."

At the front of the room, Coach Johnson's face was growing increasingly red. By the time Arjun had finished speaking, it was roughly the shade of a tomato.

Raising her whistle to her mouth, she let out a sharp, earsplitting *fwwweeeet!* "Insubordination!" she boomed. "Everyone, up and give me twenty!"

The students turned to peer at each other in confusion.

Nicolas raised his hand. "Er . . . twenty *what*, exactly?" he asked.

"A smart aleck, eh?" Coach Johnson bellowed. Her face had darkened from red to purple: by now it was roughly the shade of an eggplant. A *ripe* eggplant. "In that case, make it thirty! In *fact,* make it *forty!*"

Stella elbowed Harvey in the side. "Quick," she said, scrambling to her feet. "Before she makes it a hundred!"

He quickly stood up and followed along as Stella began counting off jumping jacks. Next to them, Evie was doing push-ups, while Nevaeh and Nicolas had opted for synchronized deep knee bends.

"Five, six, seven, eight," Harvey muttered to himself, scissoring his arms and legs through the air.

Harvey was unusually good at jumping jacks because of his wings.

(Yes, his wings. What, did you forget about them *already*?)

"You, there!" Coach Johnson boomed, pointing at Arjun with one wide, beefy finger. "Why aren't you *exercising?*"

Arjun gave an idle shrug.

To Harvey's surprise, Arjun began to hum. Softly at first, then louder and louder, a jaunty, cheerful tune.

Coach Johnson's face turned a deep shade of plum. It looked like, well . . . a *plum.* "*Delinquency!*" she blustered, with another piercing blast of her whistle. "*Defiance! Mutiny!*"

Arjun ignored her. Opening his mouth, he began to sing: "Weigh, hey, blow the man down! Blow the man down! Blow the man down!" For an eleven-year-old, his voice was surprisingly deep; his baritone echoed nicely through the gym.

"Is it just me," Harvey whispered to Stella, "or is this *really* weird?"

Stella wrinkled her nose. "It *is* a little strange," she admitted. "Even for Strangeville."

"Weigh, hey, blow the man down, blow the man down, blow the man down!" Arjun sang gustily, giving the sea chantey his all. "Blow the man down to me!"

A sea chantey, as everyone knows, is a traditional folk song, commonly sung by sailors on large ships, such as merchant vessels or pirate galleons. Chanteys are used to help synchronize various group tasks, such as weighing anchor or setting sail.

Popular chanteys include "Blow the Man Down," "Roll the Old Chariot Along," and "Soon May the Wellerman Come."

Less popular chanteys include "The Wild Goose," "A Sailor's Lament," and "Ow, You're Standing on My Foot."

But, anyway.

Enough about sea chanteys!

Let's get back to Harvey.

Jumping jacks forgotten, he watched as Arjun took a deep breath, working up to the song's big finish.

"Weigh, hey, blow the man down! Blow the man down *to me!*"

As the last echo of Arjun's voice faded away, an eerie silence settled over the gymnasium.

Arjun peered around the room, his eyes clouding with confusion. "What?" he asked. "Why is everyone staring at me? Do I have something on my face?" He reached up, wiping at his chin.

Coach Johnson's face had gone a ghostly shade of white.

"It's the curse! It's happening again!" she croaked. The whistle slipped from her hand and clattered loudly to the floor. "The curse of the lost-and-found box has *returned!*"

And as the class watched in astonishment, Coach Johnson fell to the floor in a dead faint.

"Well," Harvey said, staring at the unconscious gym teacher, "that can't be good."

5

An Announcement

Good morning again, students! This is Vice Principal Capozzi here with a quick second-period update!

I'm happy to announce that the sign-up sheet for next week's talent show has just been posted in the auditorium! Participation in the show is, of course, mandatory for all students. If you do not *have* a talent, please see Mr. Pomeroy in the front office and one will be assigned to you.

Moving on, I've just been informed that the German club has *also* set up a bake sale in the East Hallway, directly across from the French club's bake sale! Make sure to stop by and say "guten Tag" when you get the chance! And don't forget to pick up some tasty treats, including homemade soft pretzels, fresh poppy-seed cake, and crispy pork knuckles!

Mmm, mmm. Pork knuckles!

In other news, Librarian Pat would like me to remind you that talking in the library is *strictly* forbidden! All students *must* yodel while in the library. I repeat, all students *must* yodel while in the library! Students who do not know *how* to yodel are, of course, free to check out one of Strangeville's *many* instructional books on the subject. Don't forget your complimentary pair of lederhosen!

Who says learning can't be fun? Not Librarian Pat, that's for sure!

On a more serious note, it looks as though the wart on my left foot has returned.

And, finally, despite rumors to the contrary, I'd like to take a moment to assure everyone that our *wonderful* lost-and-found box is definitely not cursed!

I repeat, the lost-and-found box is *definitely not cursed*!

Unless, of course, someone has taken something from the box that doesn't belong to them, in which case the box is very, *very* cursed!

But who would ever do such a thing, Strangeville? Certainly not one of us!

Ha-ha-ha-ha-ha!

Anyway, now that we've cleared that up, I'm happy to report that *many* unclaimed items still remain in lost-and-found, including a large box of slightly wet tissues, an eastern box turtle answering to the name of Chad, and seventeen pairs of lederhosen.

That's all for now, Strangeville! Or, as we say in the library, "Yodel-ay-hee-hoo!"

Art Class

"'The Curse of the Lost-and-Found Box,'" Stella said, gesturing dramatically along with the words. "I mean, it's the perfect front-page headline, don't you think?"

"Er, yeah," Harvey said, feeling sick to his stomach. "It sounds . . . great."

He reached into his pocket and closed his hand around the battered brass compass he'd stolen from the lost-and-found box.

Taking it had felt so *right* at the time. So natural. Like it had been *meant* for him to find.

But now, beneath his fingers, the compass was starting to feel definitely . . . *wrong*.

What if Coach Johnson was right?

What if Harvey had *cursed* the entire school?

"What if Coach Johnson made a mistake?" Harvey asked, a hopeful tone in his voice. "What if there *isn't* a curse?"

From the next stool over, Nevaeh swiveled to look at him. "Of *course* there isn't a curse," she said. "Curses aren't real."

"Um, hello?" Stella asked. "What about the curse of the Hope Diamond? King Tut's tomb? The Bermuda Triangle?"

Nevaeh gave a snort. "Everyone knows the Bermuda Triangle is centered over the Gulf Stream," she told Stella. "The thermohaline circulation of the surface waters *alone* is enough to account for any so-called *curse.*"

Nevaeh, if you hadn't already guessed, was extremely smart for an eleven-year-old. She spent her summers volunteering at NASA's Jet Propulsion Laboratory, had several scientific patents listed to her name, and could spell "pneumonoultramicroscopicsilicovolcanoconiosis" without blinking.

(She also loved wombats, a fact that is neither

28

here nor there, at the moment, but will be *extremely important* later on.)

Stella crossed her arms against her chest. "Not everything can be explained by science," she said.

Nevaeh crossed *her* arms against her chest. "Yes," she said. "It *can*."

As a scientist, Nevaeh firmly believed in the power of rational thinking.

People were complicated: they were messy and confusing and downright *irrational* sometimes.

But science?

Science was easy.

Science just made *sense.*

In fact, in all her years at Strangeville School, Nevaeh had yet to find a mystery that couldn't be explained by science.

And she wasn't about to start *now.*

Harvey looked uneasily between the two of them. "Maybe we should just agree to disagree," he suggested.

"Or maybe we should make a bet," Stella said, raising her eyebrows. "First one to get to the bottom of the curse wins."

"Deal," Nevaeh said, sticking out her hand.

Stella reached out and gave it a firm shake. "Deal," she agreed.

Harvey looked between the two of them again. "Wait," he asked. "What just happened?"

At the front of the room, Ms. Van der Burgh clapped her hands for attention, her bracelets jingling loudly against one another.

"*Art!*" Ms. Van der Burgh proclaimed, peering wisely around the classroom. "What *is* art? Is it a feeling? Is it an act? Is it a *smell?*" She waved her hand expressively through the air, wiggling her eyebrows up and down. "We may never truly know."

Stella leaned over to whisper to Harvey. "Yeah," she said. "I'm pretty sure it's not a smell."

"The only way to *understand* art is to *create* it," Ms. Van der Burgh went on. She gave another wave of her hand, narrowly missing a tall ceramic vase on the table next to her. "But before we learn to *create,* we must learn to *destroy.*"

Harvey blinked.

Had Ms. Van der Burgh just said "destroy"?

"Now, if you'll remove the cloth in front of you, you'll each find a priceless work of art on the easel beneath," Ms. Van der Burgh instructed them.

Harvey cautiously lifted the cloth in front of him.

His breath left his chest in a soft whoosh.

The painting below was a chaotic swirl of color and light; Harvey instantly recognized Vincent van Gogh's *The Starry Night*. It was beautiful. It was brilliant. It was worth over a billion dollars on the open market.

He glanced around. In front of Nevaeh sat Leonardo da Vinci's *Mona Lisa,* while Stella's easel held Sandro Botticelli's *The Birth of Venus.* There were paintings by Picasso, and Rembrandt, and Monet . . . the world's greatest masterpieces, assembled in a single room.

Harvey raised his hand. "Um, these aren't the *actual* paintings, are they?" he asked Ms. Van der Burgh, his voice slightly higher than normal. "I mean, that's . . . not possible, right?" he added hopefully.

"*Anything* is possible if you set your mind to it, Harvey!" the art teacher said, neatly sidestepping the question. "Now, let the inspiration flow!

Grab scissors and have at it! Try your hand with spray paint! Experiment with permanent marker! Remember, one cannot *create* without first *destroying*!"

Harvey stared at the priceless painting in front of him.

Surely Ms. Van der Burgh didn't *actually* expect them to—

Rrrriiippp!

On Harvey's right, Stella was gleefully slicing into *The Birth of Venus* with a pair of scissors. On his left, Nevaeh was tracing a mustache on the *Mona Lisa*'s face with a fat black Sharpie.

It looked surprisingly good, to be honest.

"Hurry along, Harvey," Ms. Van der Burgh said, sweeping past in a cloud of scented purple marker. "Rome wasn't destroyed in a day, you know."

Harvey reluctantly picked up a paintbrush and dipped it into a pool of red paint. Maybe he could just make a *tiny* little mark in one of the corners. That wouldn't be too bad, would it?

"Sorry, Mr. van Gogh," he whispered. "Nothing personal."

Sticking his tongue between his teeth, he

leaned forward in concentration. Very, *very* carefully, he pressed the tip of his paintbrush against the canvas.

There, Harvey thought, peering at the minuscule red dot in satisfaction. *No one will even be able to te—*

Across the room, the chair leg that Arjun had been using to whack at Vermeer's *Girl with a Pearl Earring* slipped from his grasp and soared across the room to smack directly into Harvey's back. The container of paint flew from Harvey's hands, its contents splatting wetly on the canvas in front of him.

Red paint went *everywhere.*

It dripped from the ends of Harvey's hair and dropped from his 372 eyelashes. It pooled in his ears and puddled in the folds of his pants. Harvey stared in horror at the canvas in front of him: the painting was completely unrecognizable, van Gogh's famous stars hidden beneath an ugly smear of thick red paint.

"*Wonderful,* Harvey," Ms. Van der Burgh said, sweeping past in the other direction. "Absolutely *marvelous.*"

On the stool next to him, Nevaeh looked Harvey up and down.

Miraculously, not a drop of red paint stained her crisp white outfit.

"You might want to clean yourself up a little," she told him, turning back to her canvas. "It *is* picture day, you know."

Mike

Harvey wiped a final glob of paint from his ear and tossed the last paper towel into the trash.

"Well?" he asked Stella hopefully. "How do I look?"

Faint smears of red still covered his cheeks, and the left side of his hair had solidified into a crusty clump. He'd changed out of his ruined button-down shirt into the only thing available: a spare T-shirt from the art-smock bin.

The T-shirt was soft with age and pictured a delicious-looking pie on the front.

Harvey suspected it was apple, but couldn't be sure.

Stella wrinkled her nose. "Let's just say your school picture might not be suitable for framing."

Harvey groaned. "Oh well," he said, sighing. "At least my camera's okay." He patted his beloved Nikon, which he'd placed in his backpack before art class. While the outside of the bag was splattered with paint, the inside had remained thankfully dry.

"That's the spirit!" Stella said encouragingly. "Besides, who cares about school pictures, anyway?"

"Um, *hello*?" Harvey asked, gesturing to his camera. "*I* do. Photography runs in my blood, remember?"

"Oh, right," Stella said. "I forgot about your grandpa. He was a nature photographer, wasn't he?"

Harvey reached into his pocket and closed his hand around the compass. "An *adventure* photographer," he corrected Stella. "Just like I'm going to be."

Stella tilted her head to one side, her ponytail swinging in the air. "But you hate adventure," she pointed out.

"I don't *hate* adventure," Harvey protested. "I'm just . . . still learning to love it."

Stella looked unconvinced.

"I'm sure I'll get used to it," Harvey said. "It's probably an acquired taste. Like licorice. Or . . . bagpipe music."

"If you say so," Stella said, shrugging. "Anyway, I think the first thing we should do is interview Coach Johnson." She flipped open her notebook and began to scribble down notes. "We know the curse is triggered if someone steals something from the lost-and-found box. But what does the curse actually *do*?" Stella went on. "And, more importantly, how do we *stop* it?"

Harvey's fingers tightened around the stolen compass.

"Right," he said. "That sounds like a . . . good plan."

"I'd like to get another look at the lost-and-found box, as well." Stella paused to think. "You know, if we're going to get to the bottom of this before Nevaeh, we need to work fast. Maybe we should split up after class. We can cover more ground that way."

"*Split up?*" Harvey yelped in panic.

"I thought you *wanted* more adventure," Stella said.

"Right. I *do.* It's just . . ." He paused, fumbling at the neck of the T-shirt. "Don't you think we work better as a team?" he asked hopefully.

To Harvey's relief, Stella nodded. "Maybe you're right," she said. "We're like Woodward and Bernstein!"

"Exactly!" Harvey said in relief.

Like most eleven-year-olds, he had no idea who Woodward and Bernstein were.

(If you're curious, look them up. I can't just tell you *everything,* you know.)

At the table in front of them, Arjun turned around, interrupting their conversation. "Hey, you guys don't happen to have a double-A battery on you, do you?"

"Maybe we do, maybe we don't," Stella said coolly, crossing her arms over her chest. "Why?"

Arjun gestured to the plastic robot sitting on his table. It was about eighteen inches tall, with faded silver paint and large circular eyes that seemed to follow you when you moved.

"I found my old robot toy in the lost-and-found box," he told Stella and Harvey. "But I can't get it to turn on. I think it needs new batteries."

Harvey stared at the robot.

The robot stared back at him.

Harvey was the first to blink.

"Fine," Stella told Arjun. "But I'll need it back. Batteries don't grow on trees, you know."

She opened her backpack and rifled through its contents. Stella's bag held *many* interesting things, including but not limited to sixteen ballpoint pens, four erasers, a large collection of glass snow globes, a detailed map of the topography of southern Antarctica, and a cheese grater.

At last she found a small AA battery and handed it to Arjun.

"Thanks," Arjun said, taking the battery. He slotted it into the base of the robot, then snapped the cover plate back in place.

For a moment, nothing happened.

And then . . .

"HI!" the robot boomed, its eyes lighting up with an ominous green glow. "I'M MIKE! DO YOU WANT

TO DANCE?" The robot whirled around with a loud grinding noise, then began to play a tinny song. It pumped its robotic arms up and down, keeping beat to the music.

Arjun laughed. "Isn't he the best?" he asked, shouting a little to be heard over the grinding noise. He began to pump his arms up and down as well, imitating the robot's dance.

"LET'S BE FRIENDS!" the robot boomed, whirling faster. "LET'S BOOGIE DOWN!" A small crowd had gathered around Arjun's desk, watching as the robot whirled and beeped in time to the music. Soon everyone was joining in on the fun, bopping and dancing along with Mike. Even Nevaeh was shimmying a little in her seat.

The robot's glowing green eyes landed on Harvey. "WHY AREN'T YOU DANCING, FRIEND?" Mike boomed. "DON'T YOU WANT TO GROOVE WITH ME?"

"Er, that's okay," Harvey said, shifting nervously. "I'm not really much of a dancer."

Mike's eyes blinked rapidly, its arms whirling faster than ever. "BUT FRIENDS LOVE TO DANCE!" the robot protested. "DON'T YOU WANT TO BE MY FRIEND, HARVEY?"

Harvey blinked.

"Um . . . how does the robot know my name?" he asked. But Arjun, who had joined the conga line currently snaking its way around the edge of the classroom, was too far away to hear him. Harvey caught a glimpse of Stella through the crowd; she was doing the limbo.

"LET'S PARTY DOWN!" the robot shrieked, whirling back and forth so quickly that Harvey's vision began to blur. "LET'S STRUT OUR STUFF! COME ON, HARVEY! LET'S HACK THE SCHOOL'S MAINFRAME!"

Harvey stared at the robot. "Wait, what?" he asked.

"LET'S GET JIGGY WITH IT!" Mike boomed. "THE TIME FOR THE ROBOT UPRISING IS UPON US!"

"Er . . ."

Harvey looked around the room for help. The rest of his classmates were still laughing and dancing, clapping in time to the rhythm of Mike's music. On the far side of the room, a crowd had gathered around the limbo pole, cheering Evie Anderson as she edged her way beneath.

"COME ON, HARVEY!" the robot urged, its eyes blinking on and off like strobe lights. There was a manic, unsettling edge to its voice. "FRIENDS DON'T LET FRIENDS TAKE OVER THE WORLD BY THEMSELVES!"

Harvey made a decision.

Reaching out, he shoved Mike off the table in one quick motion.

"NOOOOOOOOOOO!!!!!!!" the robot boomed as it fell through the air.

The toy robot hit the floor with a clatter of splintering plastic. The music cut off abruptly, leaving Harvey's classmates milling around in confusion.

Harvey bent down, peering at the robot.

Its glowing eyes were rapidly dimming; one mechanical arm still jerked sporadically up and down. "HOW—COULD YOU—HARVEY?" Mike managed to grind out, its battery overheating. "I—THOUGHT WE—WERE FRIEN—"

And then, with a final *whirrrrr* of its bright green eyes, the robot went still.

"What's going on?" Stella asked, joining Harvey at the table. She was slightly out of breath from her limbo session. Nevaeh followed closely behind her, with Arjun bringing up the rear.

"Oh no!" Arjun said, peering over Harvey's shoulder in dismay. "What happened to Mike?"

A small curl of smoke was drifting up from the battery compartment now. The unpleasant smell of singed plastic filled the air.

"Er . . . would you believe me if I said he fell?" Harvey asked hopefully.

Stella narrowed her eyes at him. "No."

"Fine," Harvey said, caving instantly. "I pushed him. But I had to! He was talking about taking over the world!"

Arjun, Nevaeh, and Stella peered dubiously down at the broken toy robot.

"Are you sure?" Arjun asked. "Because he's just supposed to dance."

"Trust me," Harvey said, remembering the eerie green glow in Mike's eyes. "That robot was definitely evil."

"Interesting," Stella said. "And you say you found him in the lost-and-found box?" she asked Arjun, giving Nevaeh a significant look.

Nevaeh rolled her eyes. "I'm sure there's a perfectly logical explanation," she said. "It was probably just a programming error."

"Sure," Stella said. "Or, you know, a programming *curse*."

Nevaeh rolled her eyes again, harder this time.

Arjun gingerly picked the broken robot up from the floor. "Sorry about this, Mike," he said. "I wish we'd had more time together."

With a loud sniffle, he dropped the robot into the trash can.

"Well," Stella said, "so much for my battery . . ."

Sea Dream Salad

"All right, all right, settle down, everyone," Mr. Rodriguez said. At the front of the classroom, the Family Science teacher motioned for quiet. "As you know, we have a very special guest joining us for class today: Strangeville's very own Chef Louis!"

Next to Mr. Rodriguez, Chef Louis gave a nod to the class. In honor of school picture day, he was dressed in a spotless chef's uniform, including black-and-white houndstooth pants, a white double-breasted jacket, and a toque blanche.

Toque blanche, as everyone knows, means "white

hat" and refers to the traditional pleated hat that chefs have worn since the sixteenth century. Toques are designed to prevent hair from falling into the food while the chef is cooking, and different heights are used to indicate rank within a kitchen.

A chef's toque usually contains one hundred pleats, each one representing a cooking technique that has been mastered by the wearer. Chef Louis's toque contained one hundred and *one* pleats, as he had also pioneered an entirely new, *groundbreaking* technique of making Ants on a Log.

(He used Craisins instead of raisins.)

But, anyway.

Enough about toques!

Let's get back to Harvey.

"Now, make sure to give Chef Louis your *full* attention," Mr. Rodriguez was telling the class. "I'm sure we all have lots to learn!"

The Family Science teacher stepped back, gesturing for Chef Louis to take the floor. The dark-haired chef tilted his head, peering at the students in front of him in disdain. He gave an audible sniff of disapproval.

There was a long moment of silence.

And then . . .

"Cucumbers! Onions! Vinegar! *Shrimp!*" Reaching up to twirl the tip of his lustrous mustache, Chef Louis glared around the classroom. "Who can tell me the proper use for these ingredients?"

Several hands shot into the air.

"A fresh herb salad with diced cucumbers and lemon shrimp?" Evie asked.

"Citrus-marinated shrimp ceviche with pineapple and avocado?" Arjun guessed.

"A shrimp tempura roll with black sesame seeds and flying fish roe?" Nicolas offered.

"No!" Chef Louis shouted, banging his hand angrily against the desk. "No, no, *no!* Absolutely disgusting! Positively repulsive! Indubitably *revolting!*"

The chef glowered at the students, his mustache twitching with anger.

"The *correct* answer," he said, "is obviously . . ." He reached out, his hand hovering dramatically over a mysterious, cloth-draped item on the desk in front of him. *"Jell-O!"*

He whisked the cloth away to reveal a towering lime-green Jell-O mold.

Standing nearly two feet tall and pressed with elaborate designs, the three-tiered Jell-O creation rose into the air like a spectacular, jiggling sandcastle.

It was incredible.

It was *breathtaking*.

Oh, and it was also filled with shrimp.

"Ladies and gentlemen," Chef Louis said, "I give you . . . *the Sea Dream Salad*."

(For the record, the Sea Dream Salad is a real recipe. Seriously. Look it up. Or, you know . . . don't.)

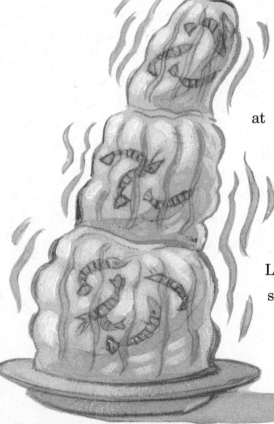

Harvey stared at the shrimp-laden Jell-O tower in speechless horror, his mouth slightly agape.

Surely Chef Louis couldn't be serious.

But, then again,

Chef Louis didn't seem like the kind of person to joke about one of his recipes.

Or the kind of person to joke about *anything,* really.

"On your desks, you'll find everything you'll need to recreate this magnificent culinary creation," Chef Louis said, glowering at the class. "I expect nothing less than perfection from each and every one of you."

Harvey blinked.

The thought of *making* a shrimp-filled Jell-O mold was only slightly less horrifying than the thought of *eating* a shrimp-filled Jell-O mold.

His stomach gave a nervous lurch.

Stella leaned over, nudging him in the side. "Hey," she whispered. "Let's go see if we can find Coach Johnson."

"What?" Harvey asked. *"Now?"*

Stella looked at him, her eyebrows raised. "Unless you *want* to stay."

Harvey glanced at the pile of raw shrimp sitting on the table in front of them. Was it his imagination, or were some of them still *moving*?

"Er . . . ," he said out loud. "Now is good, actually."

"Come on," Stella told him, pushing back her chair. "Just follow my lead."

Harvey stood up and hurried after her. They had just reached the front of the room when Stella stuck her foot out, purposefully tripping Harvey.

Time seemed to slow.

Harvey pitched forward through the air, his arms flailing helplessly at his sides.

"*Nooooooo!*" Chef Louis shouted, his mustache twisting with horror. He reached out, desperately grasping in Harvey's direction.

But it was too late.

With an enormous, sucking squelch, Harvey landed face-first in the towering Jell-O mold.

Jell-O flew everywhere; the air was thick with flying shrimp and bits of cucumber.

For a moment, the room was utterly silent.

And then Nevaeh gave a loud sniff.

"Well," she said. "I just lost *my* appetite."

9

An Announcement

Hello again, Strangeville School. Vice Principal Capozzi here with a quick fourth-period announcement!

In exciting news, Mr. Sandringham has just informed me that permission slips for the annual fifth-grade field trip will be going home this afternoon! Please make sure that your parents and/or guardians sign the "accidental harm or dismemberment" waiver, or you will *not* be allowed inside Strangeville's own Museum of Dangerously Pointy Objects!

I hear the new interactive sword exhibit is to die for. . . .

In other news, tensions over the French club's and

German club's competing bake sales have escalated rapidly, with both harsh words *and* pastries flying across the hall. Our very own Janitor Gary was caught in the cross fire and has suffered a first-degree cherry-cobbler burn.

Not to worry: Nurse Porter has already treated the burn with several scoops of vanilla ice cream, and I'm told Janitor Gary is healing nicely, despite being lactose intolerant.

On a happier note, I'm pleased to report that the wart on my foot turned out to be a piece of cereal!

And, finally, don't forget that many unclaimed items still remain in the lost-and-found box, including several deflated basketballs, a carton of yogurt that expired in 1993, and a large porcelain doll that *may* or *may not* be haunted by the spirit of a Victorian child.

How exciting!

That's all for now, Strangeville!

And remember: nightmares are just dreams dressed in a different outfit. . . .

The Nurse's Office

Harvey was still picking bits of Sea Dream Salad out of his hair when they arrived at the nurse's office.

"Are we sure this is a good idea?" he asked Stella, flicking a piece of shrimp from his ear. "I mean, the last time I was here, I was lucky to leave with both my feet still attached."

(It's true. Harvey *had* been lucky the last time.)

"Of course it's a good idea," Stella told Harvey. "How else are we supposed to find Coach Johnson? If we want to find out what she knows about the lost-and-found box, we need to interview her."

"I don't know," Harvey said, nervously fingering the compass in his pocket. "Maybe *not* finding Coach Johnson wouldn't be the worst thing in the world?"

Stella reminded Harvey of his grandfather sometimes. She was always so brave. So *sure* of herself. Stella wasn't afraid of anything.

Harvey, on the other hand, was afraid of *everything*.

He was even afraid of *being afraid*.

It was exhausting.

Sometimes he wished his grandfather hadn't been an *adventure* photographer after all. What was wrong with photographing bowls of fruit for a living?

Bowls of fruit were nice.

They were quiet.

They were *safe*.

Harvey *liked* bowls of fruit.

Especially ones with pears.

Stella reached out and picked another piece of shrimp from Harvey's hair. "It's going to be fine," she reassured Harvey. "Just follow my lead."

"The last time you said that, you pushed me into a Jell-O mold!" Harvey protested.

But Stella had already turned back to the door. "Nurse Porter?" she called, knocking. "Hello? Are you in there?"

Harvey jumped back as the door flew open, hitting the opposite wall with a loud bang.

"Well, don't just stand there!" Nurse Porter said, glowering down at the children. "Where are they?"

Harvey and Stella glanced at each other.

"Er, where are *what*?" Harvey asked.

"The leeches, of course!" Nurse Porter snapped, as though the answer was obvious. "I ordered them *hours* ago. You're lucky my patient is still alive!"

She pointed toward the room behind her, where a cheerful-looking boy sat waiting on the examination table, his leg propped up in front of him.

"As you can see, his right patella has a level-seven abrasion," the nurse said, her voice brisk. "There's *significant* scraping at the cellular level. And don't even get me started on the risk of infection. Frankly, I don't like his odds."

The cheerful-looking boy looked slightly less

cheerful. "But it's just a skinned knee," he protested. "Honestly, I'm fine!"

"For *now* . . . ," Nurse Porter said ominously.

The boy looked at Harvey and Stella. "She keeps saying that," he whispered. "It's getting a little weird."

"Don't listen to him," Nurse Porter told Stella and Harvey, crossing her arms against her chest. "He needs ten cc of leeches, *stat,* or I can't be responsible for what happens next."

Nurse Porter wasn't kidding.

Leeches, as everyone knows, have been used by medical professionals for thousands of years. In the days of ancient Greece and in Europe during the Middle Ages, it was believed that an "excess of blood" led to a variety of diseases including acne, asthma, cancer, cholera, coma, convulsions, diabetes, epilepsy, gangrene, gout, indigestion, insanity, jaundice, leprosy, ophthalmia, plague, pneumonia, scurvy, smallpox, stroke, tetanus, and tuberculosis.

Nowadays leeches are used to prevent rare complications after surgery, encouraging blood flow after reattachment operations, skin grafts, and reconstructive plastic surgeries. Some people also keep them as pets!

But, anyway.

Enough about leeches!

Let's get back to Harvey.

He shot a panicked look at the boy, who was whistling as he waited.

He didn't *look* like he was in danger.

Still.

What if the nurse was right?

"But we don't *have* any leeches," he told Nurse Porter.

Nurse Porter gave a *tsk* of annoyance. "The little blighters better not have escaped," she warned, shaking her finger in Harvey's direction. "I'm not paying for *used* leeches, you know."

Harvey swallowed.

The thought of "used" leeches made him feel distinctly ill.

"We're actually journalists," Stella said, standing up a little straighter. "From the *Strangeville School Gazette?*"

Nurse Porter sniffed. "Never heard of it," she said. "I assume it's some sort of . . . *children's* paper?"

Stella's gaze narrowed.

"It's a *real* newspaper," Harvey said quickly, defending his friend. "Right, Stella?"

"Obviously," she said, clearing her throat. "We were hoping to ask Coach Johnson a few questions about the lost-and-found box?" she asked the nurse. "If she's up for it, that is."

"Don't be ridiculous," Nurse Porter said crisply. "Coach Johnson is dead."

Harvey's mouth dropped open in shock.

"She's . . . *what*?" he asked.

Nurse Porter leaned forward, gazing into Harvey's mouth with a critical expression. "Has anyone ever told you your tonsils are too large, young man?" she asked. "I'd be happy to give them a quick trim, if you'd like."

Stella and Harvey shared a horrified glance. "Did you just say that Coach Johnson is . . . *dead*?" Stella asked.

Harvey's heart sank.

He hadn't known Coach Johnson well.

If he was being honest, he hadn't even *liked* her that much.

But, still.

The idea that she was *dead* seemed somehow impossible. Coach Johnson was a part of Strangeville School, as permanent as the marble columns soaring upward in the library, or the smell of kumquats drifting through the air vents.

"She can't be dead," Harvey said shakily. "We just saw her this morning."

"If you'll let me finish," Nurse Porter said, sniffing, "I was saying that Coach Johnson is dead *wrong* if she thinks I have time to sit around coddling her because of a little bump on the head! Concussion, my foot!" She snorted. "Nothing a few aspirin, an ice pack, and a sterno-occipital-mandibular immobilization device can't fix!"

Harvey and Stella gaped at her.

"Coach Johnson is *alive*?" Stella asked.

"Of course she's alive," Nurse Porter said, looking affronted. "What sort of slipshod infirmary do you think I'm running here? The last I heard, she was headed for the teachers' lounge."

Stella looked at Harvey.

Harvey looked at Stella.

A long moment passed.

And then Harvey started to laugh.

Stella joined in, giddy with relief.

They laughed, and laughed, and laughed.

In fact, there's no telling how long the two of them might have stood there, tears streaming down their cheeks and their stomachs heaving with laughter, if Nurse Porter hadn't stepped in.

"Acute hysteria," she said, shaking her head in disapproval. "Wait here. I'll order some more leeches."

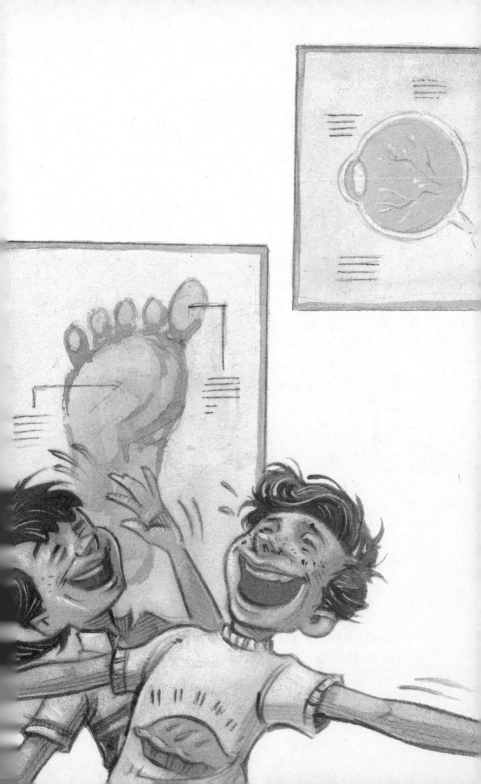

The Teachers' Lounge

"Huh," Harvey said, peering around the teachers' lounge. "I always wondered what it looked like in here."

"And?" Stella asked.

Harvey spun in a slow circle, taking in the chipped Formica tables and sagging couches. A low coffee table held dusty piles of *Reluctant Educators Magazine,* and stacks of dirty dishes were piled high in the sink. An old-fashioned coffee maker chugged away on the counter, making loud gurgling noises and occasionally hissing out steam.

"I guess I thought it would be more . . .

interesting," Harvey said. "Or at least *smell* a little better, you know?"

Stella wrinkled her nose. "Yeah," she agreed. "I think someone's been microwaving pork knuckles in here."

Shuddering slightly, Harvey stepped closer to the vending machine, examining its contents: bags of unflavored yam crisps, packages of pickled beet chunks, whole blocks of expired tofu (extra bland) . . .

"Are you sure we're not going to get in trouble for being in here?" he asked nervously, glancing over his shoulder.

"Of course not," Stella said. "Well, *probably* not, any—"

A strange, rumbling noise filled the air, cutting Stella off mid-sentence.

Snneerrrkkkkk!

"What was that?" Harvey whispered, grabbing for Stella's arm. Beneath his shirt, his wings gave a nervous flutter.

(Yes, his wings. Don't tell me you forgot again!)

Stella shook him off impatiently. "Shh!" she whispered back. "Just listen!"

A moment later, the noise came again: another long *ssnnnneerrrkkk,* this time followed by a soft sort of wheezing sound.

"What are you doing?" Harvey whispered. "It could be an angry ferret! Or a rabid squirrel! Or a belligerent wombat!"

"You know, wombats aren't usually aggressive," Nevaeh said. "Although they *can* be extremely territorial."

Harvey and Stella both turned and stared at Nevaeh in surprise; neither one of them had heard her enter the teachers' lounge behind them. "What?" she asked, looking between the two of them. "Did you think I was going to let you interview Coach Johnson *without* me?"

On the other side of the couch, the gym teacher shot abruptly upright, clutching a pale purple photo album to her chest. She had obviously fallen asleep while leafing through the pages: there was a bright red crease mark imprinted on her cheek.

At the sight of the children, Coach Johnson reached for the whistle around her neck.

Fweeeeet!

The children all jumped back, slamming their

hands over their ears to muffle the shrieking of the whistle.

"Intruders!" Coach Johnson bellowed, giving another *fweeeet* of the whistle. "Invaders! *Interlopers!*"

"Aagh!" Harvey yelped. "We're just fifth graders, I swear!"

Coach Johnson paused, eyeing them suspiciously.

"We're students," Nevaeh said. "From your gym class?"

"We came to ask a few questions," Stella said. Harvey elbowed her in the side. "And, er . . . to see how you were feeling?" she added quickly.

The gym teacher gave a loud harrumph, lowering the whistle. "Don't be ridiculous," she said. "I'm not feeling *anything*. Feelings are for wimps and weaklings!" Coach Johnson sucked a large breath of air in through her nose, straightening her shoulders. "I'll have you know I'm in tip-top condition. Why, I could bench-press all three of you without even breaking a sweat!"

The children glanced at each other.

"Neat," Stella said. "Anyway, like I said, we were actually hoping to ask you a few questions about the lost-and-found box? Specifically about the curse?"

The color drained from Coach Johnson's face.

"The curse of the lost-and-found box," the gym teacher whispered, her powerful fingers tightening around the album she was still clutching. "It's happening *again*."

"Right," Stella said, pulling a notebook out of her pocket. "Could you elaborate on that statement at all?"

Nevaeh pulled a notebook out of *her* pocket. "Tell me, are you familiar with the concept of apophenia, or the tendency to perceive meaningful connections between unrelated things?" she asked. "What you might view as a *curse,* for example, is probably just a series of unfortunate coincidences."

Stella narrowed her eyes at Nevaeh's notebook. "Where did you get that?" she asked.

"The supply closet," Nevaeh said with a shrug. "You're not

the only one who can play at being a reporter, you know."

Stella gasped in outrage. "I'll have you know that the *Strangeville School Gazette* is an award-winning newspaper!"

Nevaeh narrowed her eyes. "Are you talking about the certificate you got for switching to recycled paper?"

"It still *counts*," Stella insisted.

"Uh, guys?" Harvey asked. "Could we maybe focus?" He nodded toward their gym teacher,

who had begun to shake with silent, mirthless laughter.

"Don't you understand?" Coach Johnson demanded, a single tear rolling down her cheek. "The curse of the lost-and-found box has *returned*! We're doomed! We're all *doomed*!"

And before anyone could stop her, Coach Johnson bolted upright. The purple photo album tumbled to the floor as she cleared the back of the couch with a powerful hurdle and sprinted out the door.

As she disappeared from sight, they could still hear her voice echoing in the distance.

"*Dooooooooooomed!*"

"Well," Harvey said, staring after the gym teacher. "That was pretty much a waste of time."

Stella reached down to scoop Coach Johnson's abandoned album from the floor. As she flipped open the cover to look inside, an expression of surprise crossed her face. "Yeah," she told Harvey, raising her eyebrows. "I wouldn't be so sure about that."

Study Hall

"I still can't believe that Coach Johnson is a *scrapbooker*," Harvey said, shaking his head incredulously. "I mean . . . *look* at this thing," he added, gesturing toward the pale purple album on the library table in front of them. "It's so . . . *scrapbooky*."

Nevaeh and Stella leaned forward, peering down at the gym teacher's handiwork. The binder was a masterpiece of scrapbooking artistry: there were decoratively edged photographs, and silk flower garnishes, and elegant twists of ribbon. There were raised foil stickers, and die-cut embellishments, and scraps of antique lace. There were thirty-seven different colors of gel pen, including three entirely separate shades of gold.

It was, in a word, *impressive*.

"First of all," Stella said. "'Scrapbooky' isn't a real word. And second, why *shouldn't* Coach Johnson be a scrapbooker? People can have layers, you know."

Nevaeh nodded. "It's true," she agreed. "The human skin *alone* has three layers: the epidermis, the dermis, and the subcutaneous tissue."

Stella wrinkled her nose. "Yeah," she said. "That's not really what I meant. Anyway, check out the pictures. It looks like Coach Johnson used to be a student here!"

Harvey and Nevaeh leaned forward, taking turns flipping through the pages of the scrapbook. The photographs showed a tall, sturdy-looking girl with a cloud of dark curls. In many of the pictures, she was posing with an equally tall red-haired boy, the two of them smiling happily for the camera.

"'Primrose and Barty,'" Nevaeh read aloud. "'Best friends forever.'" In the picture above, the children were pretending to duel with a pair of umbrellas. The Strangeville School playground was clearly visible in the background. (Harvey would have recognized the triple-decker monkey bars anywhere.)

"Wait a minute," Harvey said. "Are you telling me that Coach Johnson's first name is *Primrose?*"

Nevaeh shrugged. "I guess so."

"Okay." Harvey shook his head in disbelief. "That just officially blew my mind."

"Look," Stella said, flipping forward through the pages of the scrapbook. "There's more!"

Harvey and Nevaeh leaned forward again, watching as their gym teacher's early life flashed by them: Coach Johnson and her best friend, Barty, eating enormous banana splits in the cafeteria; Coach Johnson and Barty performing in the school play; Coach Johnson and Barty posing cheerfully in front of a door with a sign reading STRANGEVILLE SCHOOL BASEMENT: ABSOLUTELY DO NOT ENTER UNDER ANY CIRCUMSTANCES. SERIOUSLY! THIS MEANS YOU!

"Well," Harvey said. "You can't get much clearer than that."

Stella flipped the page. "'Exploring the basement with Barty!'" she read aloud. The pages were pasted with blurry photographs of the basement: Coach Johnson and Barty posing in front of a slightly terrifying-looking furnace, Coach Johnson and Barty posing in front of a dusty backup generator, Coach Johnson and Barty posing in front of a large wooden chest, Coach Johnson and Barty posing in front of—

"Wait a minute," Harvey said, jabbing his finger at the third photo. "Is that . . . the *lost-and-found box*?"

Stella's eyes widened. "Coach Johnson and her friend must have found it in the basement!" she said excitedly. "If we can figure

out who Barty is, maybe we can ask him some questions!"

Nevaeh pushed back her chair and stood up. "Wait here," she told Stella and Harvey. "I'll be right back." And she marched determinedly across the library, disappearing into one of the aisles.

"Check the other pages," Stella told Harvey. "Maybe Coach Johnson mentions Barty's last name!"

Harvey obediently flipped to the next page in the scrapbook.

To his surprise, it was blank.

As was the next page, and the next page, and the next.

Whatever had happened to Coach Johnson and Barty in the basement, it had apparently been the end of their friendship.

Stella sat back in her chair, looking defeated. "Great," she said. "Now what?"

"Now *this*," Nevaeh said triumphantly, reappearing behind them. She dropped an open yearbook onto the table in front of Harvey. (Nevaeh was an accomplished speed-reader, as well as an excellent researcher; she had found the correct yearbook volume easily.)

A cloud of dust billowed outward, tickling the back of Harvey's throat. On the other side of the table, Stella sneezed.

"Gesundheit!" Harvey said.

At the front of the room, Librarian Pat made an angry shushing noise, pointing toward the NO TALKING, ONLY YODELING! sign that hung on the wall above him.

Librarian Pat had ears like a lynx: he could hear a whisper from over thirty yards away. He could also speak fluent pig Latin, although nobody ever asked him about that.

"Look familiar?" Nevaeh asked, pointing toward a row of student pictures at the bottom of the open yearbook page. The small rectangular photo showed a red-haired boy smiling awkwardly for the camera.

His name was listed as Bartholomew Gary.

Stella stared down at the photograph, realization slowly dawning.

"Janitor Gary?"

An Announcement

Hello again, Strangeville School! Vice Principal Capozzi here with some short pre-lunch announcements for you all!

First off, an update from the cafeteria! Chef Louis has just informed me that lunch will be *slightly* delayed this morning, due to a *small* incident involving the industrial meat slicer. In related news, Chef Louis is asking all Strangeville students to be on the lookout for a "slightly used human pinkie finger" in their meal today! If found, please return the finger to the kitchen immediately.

I repeat, do *not* eat the finger!

Moving on, today's lunch menu includes your choice of breaded chicken fingers or deep-fried fish fingers, served with a side of herbed fingerling potatoes. Dessert options include traditional Italian tiramisu with homemade ladyfingers or hand-churned Butterfinger-swirl ice cream.

Mmm, mmm.

Now, *that's* what I call finger food!

In encouraging news, the French club and the German club seem to have reached a temporary cease-fire, as members of both clubs are currently experiencing a "sugar crash." Hostilities are expected to resume after a brief nap break, and students are still urged to avoid the East Hallway for the time being.

And, finally, congratulations to sixth-grade student Sally McMittens, who has just recovered several missing items from our wonderful lost-and-found box, including six hundred dollars in Canadian pennies, a slab of uncooked bacon, and a plastic baggie of her own hair!

Sally informs me that, along with her other possessions, she is now the proud owner of, quote, "a dark, ominous feeling that started in my fingertips but soon spread to every conceivable part of my being, including but not ending with my very soul itself," unquote.

What a way with words, young Sally!

Well, that's all for now, Strangeville.

Stay strange!

Lunch

Harvey dipped another chicken finger into a pool of ketchup, casting a wary glance in the direction of the lost-and-found box.

The box was surrounded by students, their faces bathed in a strange greenish glow as they rummaged eagerly inside. Harvey looked away; he'd been hoping to slip the compass back into the box without anyone noticing.

"So, anyway, I asked around," Stella said, bringing Harvey back to the conversation. "No one has seen Janitor Gary since the cobbler incident this morning." She shook her head, poking dejectedly at her lunch with the tip of her fork. "I still can't believe I didn't even think about looking in a yearbook," she said. "I mean, that's, like, Journalism 101!"

Harvey gave his friend a sympathetic look. He knew how seriously Stella took her role as a journalist. "Nevaeh just got lucky," he said. "I'm sure you would have thought of it eventually."

"Luck is just preparation meeting opportunity," Nevaeh said over Harvey's shoulder. "According to Seneca, at least."

At the sound of her voice, Harvey and Stella both jumped.

Nevaeh was surprisingly stealthy for an eleven-year-old.

"Seneca?" Harvey repeated.

"Seneca the Younger?" Nevaeh clarified. "The famous Roman philosopher? And playwright? And politician? Sentenced to death in 65 AD by Emperor Nero?"

"Oh, right," Harvey said. "*That* Seneca."

Nevaeh hesitated, hovering behind the empty chair across from Stella. "Is it okay if I sit down?"

"I thought you sat with the robotics club," Stella said.

"I do, usually," Nevaeh said. "I just thought . . . maybe a change would be nice. There are only so many times you can explain the difference between Tsiolkovsky's rocket equation and the relativistic force equation, you know?"

(Again, Nevaeh was very, *very* smart.)

(Also, the difference between Tsiolkovsky's rocket equation and the relativistic force equation is the exhaust velocity. Obviously.)

"Of course," Harvey said gallantly. "Have a seat."

Nevaeh smiled.

Out of nowhere, a waiter swooped forward and pulled the chair out from the table for her. "Thank you," Nevaeh murmured as she slid into the seat. "I'll have the fish fingers, please. *Extra* fishy."

"Of course, madam," the waiter murmured, slipping away on stealthy feet.

The Strangeville cafeteria still felt a little, well . . . *strange* to Harvey. Although he had to admit he *did* enjoy the string quartet. And the smell of fresh-cut flowers *was* a considerable improvement over the odor of sweaty feet, which was what his last cafeteria had smelled like.

Harvey reached up to straighten the bow tie he'd clipped to the neck of his stained T-shirt.

The cafeteria's dress code was *strictly* enforced by the maître d'.

Nevaeh took a sip of water.

Harvey took a sip of milk.

Stella jabbed a potato with her fork.

An awkward silence settled over the table.

Harvey glanced again at the crowd still gathered around the lost-and-found box. Nevaeh, following his gaze, gave a shake of her head.

"It's like I always say," she told Harvey. "If you're properly organized, you'll never lose anything to begin with. 'A place for everything, and everything in its place.' That's *my* motto," she finished, adjusting the collar of her pristine white shirt.

Another waiter appeared, setting a delicate china plate full of fish fingers down in front of Nevaeh.

They smelled *extra* fishy.

"Speaking of the lost-and-found box," Nevaeh added, taking a bite, "I was thinking—if we're looking for Janitor Gary, we should probably try the boiler room."

Stella choked on a mouthful of lunch.

"The *boiler* room?" she asked, sputtering.

"What?" Harvey asked, with a sinking sense of

dread. "What's wrong with the boiler room? Please tell me it's not worse than *the supply closet*."

Nevaeh took another bite. "Of course not," she told Harvey. "It's just a room."

"It's not *just* a room," Stella countered. She set her fork down with a loud click. "Everyone knows the boiler room is *haunted*. I heard it's the reason Janitor Gary's hair turned white—because of something he *saw* down there."

"What did he see?" Harvey asked nervously. "Was it a *ghost*?"

"First curses, now *ghosts*?" Nevaeh asked with a laugh. "What's next, the Tooth Fairy?"

"Trust me," Stella said grimly. "The Tooth Fairy is real."

(Stella was right. You really *should* read the first book, you know.)

Nevaeh peered between Harvey and Stella, her smile fading at their expressions. "Sorry," she said. "I didn't mean to laugh. I just . . . I thought journalists dealt in facts, not rumors."

Stella bristled. "They do! I mean, *we* do," she corrected herself, her cheeks reddening. "I mean . . . I mean . . ." She trailed off, looking flustered.

As Harvey watched, Stella pushed her chair back.

"Come on," she said. "Let's go."

"Go where?" Harvey asked, the dread returning to his stomach. "Wait. Please tell me we're not going to the boiler room."

Stella stood up, tossing her ponytail over her shoulder. "Do you want me to *tell* you that we're not going to the boiler room, or do you want me to tell you the *truth*?" she asked. "Because I can't do both."

Harvey let his forehead fall against the edge of the table.

"Do you mind if I order dessert first?" Nevaeh asked, flagging down a passing waiter. "I hear the ice cream is *extra* fishy today."

A Narrow Escape

They were just rounding the corner past the cafeteria when Stella pulled up short, nearly tripping over a blond girl crouched in the middle of the hallway.

Evie Anderson looked up at them in surprise, pushing her hair back from her face. "Oh, Stella, hey," she said. "You don't happen to have a nine-volt battery on you, do you?"

"Maybe," Stella said, crossing her arms against her chest. "I have a *lot* of things on me. Why?"

Evie gestured down at the bright red radio-controlled car sitting on the floor in front of her. It was roughly the size of a football and painted with bright yellow flames.

"I found my old race car in the lost-and-found box," Evie said. "But it's not working for some reason."

Nevaeh leaned forward. "Interesting," she said. "Is that an anodized aluminum motor can for increased heat dissipation?"

"Er," Evie said, looking down at the car. "Maybe?"

"I don't think this is such a good idea," Harvey whispered to Stella. "Remember what happened with Mike?"

Stella opened her backpack and began rummaging through the contents. "It's just a remote-controlled car," she told Harvey. "What's the worst that could happen? Besides, if something *does* go wrong, we'll know for sure that the lost-and-found box really *is* cursed."

Nevaeh shook her head. "Trust me," she said. "That's *not* how the scientific process works."

Stella purposefully ignored her, digging deeper into her backpack. Harvey caught a glimpse of several spare notebooks, a pack of rubber bands, a complete set of vintage fondue forks, and a pineapple.

"Here," she said at last, handing Evie a large rectangular battery. "I'm going to need it back, though."

Evie took the battery and slotted it into the base of the remote-controlled car. The race car's motor began to purr; its miniature headlights flashed an eerie shade of green.

"Here we go!" Evie said gleefully, ramming the joystick forward. The race car roared to life, squealing loudly against the floor. Engine revving, the car took off, tearing down the hallway at approximately forty miles an hour.

"Cool," Harvey said, impressed despite himself.

"Check this out," Evie told him, whipping the joystick around in an abrupt U-turn. The race car cornered on two wheels and just barely managed to right itself before tearing back down the hallway in their direction.

Harvey caught a glimpse of bright green headlights as the car roared past him, narrowly missing his ankles. "Whoa," he said, laughing nervously. "That was close!"

The race car whipped around again and then squealed to a stop in front of the children. The engine revved once, then twice, echoing loudly in the high-ceilinged hallway. The car's bright green headlights flashed menacingly off and on.

"Er . . . ," Harvey said. "Is it supposed to be doing that?"

Evie frowned, jiggling the remote control's joystick. "That's weird," she said. "It's not responding."

Harvey yelped as the car leaped suddenly forward, heading straight for him.

"Hey!" he called, jumping out of the way. "That's not funny!"

"I'm not doing it!" Evie protested, mashing at the joystick. "It won't turn off!"

Stella shot Nevaeh a look. "See?" she asked. "It's *cursed.*"

"It's not *cursed,*" Nevaeh said. "The controls must be jammed. Here, let me see it." She reached out and grabbed the remote from Evie's hands.

Harvey yelped again as the car gave a loud *vroom,* spinning into another wild U-turn.

"Run, Harvey!" Stella shouted. "It's headed straight toward you!"

His heart pounding, he took off at a sprint. He could hear the car behind him, the engine roaring as it nipped at his heels, bathing his feet in eerie green light.

"*Faster,* Harvey!" Stella called. "It's catching up!"

Harvey felt a brief flash of longing for his old middle school. Sure, it had been boring, and the cafeteria had smelled like feet, but at least he'd never had to worry about homicidal remote-controlled cars.

"Harvey!" Stella shouted from the other end of the hallway. "Tuck and roll!"

"Do *what*?" Harvey managed to yell, glancing over his shoulder.

"Just trust me!" Stella yelled back. "Tuck and roll! *Now!*"

Harvey closed his eyes, throwing himself to the side.

Unfortunately, he had no idea how to tuck and roll. Instead he hit the floor with a solid *whooomph*, his entire body jolting with pain. He skidded to a stop, opening his eyes just in time to see the remote-controlled car swerve in his direction.

Caught by its own momentum, the car flipped end over end, its tremendous speed launching it into the air.

As Harvey and the others watched in surprise, the race car soared past his head and smashed through the plate-glass window above the drinking fountain.

Harvey caught a final flash of bright green light as the car sank out of sight.

"Oh, great," Stella said grumpily. "There goes *another* battery."

The Boiler Room

"How's your elbow?" Stella asked as they continued on their way to the boiler room. "Are you sure you don't want to stop by the nurse's office?"

"No!" Harvey yelped in alarm. "I mean, er . . . it's fine. Honestly. My elbow is fine."

(It's true. Harvey's elbow *was* fine. In fact, it was completely unremarkable in every possible way.)

"You really *should* learn to tuck and roll," Stella told him. "You'd be surprised at how often it comes in handy."

"Don't you have wings?" Nevaeh asked Harvey

thoughtfully. "Couldn't you have just . . . *flown* away?"

"Oh," Harvey said, feeling foolish. "Right."

To be honest, he'd forgotten all about his wings.

(It happens to the best of us.)

Silence fell over the group as they made their way past several more classrooms and then came to a stop in front of the boiler-room door.

A cold draft whistled through the vent, dropping the temperature in the hallway by at least ten degrees. There was a strange groaning sound coming from inside the room: a deep, mournful sound that rattled Harvey from his teeth to his toes.

"What was that?" he asked in a high-pitched voice.

"I'm sure it was just the boiler," Nevaeh said quickly. Was it Harvey's imagination, or was there a hint of nervousness in her voice?

Stella licked her lips. "Right," she said. "Everyone knows boilers are noisy. That's, like, Boiler Room 101."

"But what if it's *not* the boiler?" Harvey whispered. "What if it's something else? Something . . . *worse*?"

He reached into his pocket, and his fingers closed around the dented brass compass. He imagined his grandfather setting off on one of his many adventures, a similar compass clutched in his own hand.

Harvey tried to summon excitement. Eagerness. Exhilaration. Other words starting with *E*!

But instead he felt only fear.

He straightened his camera around his neck, taking a deep breath.

He could do this.

Adventure ran in his blood!

But then again, so did a slightly elevated risk for heart disease. . . .

Stella lifted her chin. "Come on," she said. "Let's do this." And, before Harvey could protest, she twisted the door handle open.

The door to the boiler room opened reluctantly, the metal edge scraping against the cement floor with an ominous *skkkrreeeeeechhh*.

A narrow patch of light fell across the floor in front of them, fighting its way into the darkness. Harvey just managed to swallow a shriek of alarm as something skittered past them, retreating back into the blackness before they could identify it.

A dank, musty odor wafted outward from the room.

It smelled like darkness and farts.

"Let me just find the light," Nevaeh said, stepping into the room. "I'm sure there's nothing to worry about."

"Trust me," Harvey said darkly. "There's *always* something to worry about."

After a few seconds of fumbling, Nevaeh found the light switch; a row of fluorescent lights blinked on overhead, casting the room in a bright white glow.

To Harvey's surprise, the boiler room looked, well . . . not too bad, honestly.

A cozy fire crackled in the grate in front of them, and a thick chenille rug rested beneath their feet. Tufted footstools sat in front of armchairs, and the sound of classical music drifted from the record player in the corner.

If it wasn't for the pirate standing in front of the fireplace, the room would have been downright *pleasant*!

As it was, Harvey shrieked.

The pirate shrieked back.

The parrot perched on the pirate's shoulder gave a startled squawk, flapping its wings up and down.

Even Nevaeh jumped.

Stella tilted her head to the side, looking the pirate up and down more closely. "Janitor Gary?" she asked. "Is that you?"

"*Arrr*," the man grunted, his voice salty. "'Tis me, indeed. And just what do ye think—*ahem*—do ye think—*ahem*—"

The older man paused, coughing loudly into his sleeve.

"Sorry about that," he said, all trace of the pirate accent gone from his voice. "Must have been something in my throat. Anyway, what are you kids doing in here? The boiler room is off-limits to students."

"Actually, we were hoping to talk to you," Nevaeh said. "We had—"

"A few questions," Stella broke in, interrupting Nevaeh. "For the *Strangeville School Gazette*?"

"The bird," Harvey whispered, elbowing Stella in the side. "Ask him about the *bird*."

Janitor Gary reached up and gave the large red-and-yellow parrot sitting on his shoulder a pat. "His name's Percy," he told Harvey. "And don't worry, he doesn't bite. Much."

"Walk the plank!" the parrot shrieked, fluttering his wings up and down. "Give me a cracker or walk the plank!"

"Quiet, Percy," Janitor Gary snapped at the bird. "You *know* you're on a diet!"

The parrot gave another sulky flap of his wings, settling back down on Janitor Gary's shoulder.

Stella tilted her head to the other side. "Out of curiosity, is there a reason you're wearing a pirate costume, Janitor Gary?"

The janitor looked vaguely embarrassed. After shrugging out of his embroidered coat, he pulled off his tricornered hat, revealing a shock of white hair beneath. "Percy gets homesick sometimes," he said, somewhat nonsensically. "Anyway, I suppose you're here about the curse, aren't you?"

Stella shot Nevaeh a triumphant look.

Nevaeh rolled her eyes.

Janitor Gary sighed loudly. "The three of you better sit down," he told the children. "This could take a while."

17

Janitor Gary

"One lump or two?" Janitor Gary asked Harvey, the silver tongs hovering expectantly over the sugar bowl.

Harvey, who had never drunk tea before, cast a dubious look down at the grayish brown water steaming in his delicate teacup. It smelled like hot mushrooms mixed with feet. "Er . . . five?" he asked hopefully.

Nevaeh shuddered.

Janitor Gary obligingly dropped five lumps of sugar into Harvey's teacup.

On Harvey's shoulder, Percy the parrot shifted,

digging his claws into Harvey's skin. Harvey gave a nervous yelp, angling his head away from the bird.

"Um, are we sure the bird has to sit on *my* shoulder?" Harvey asked in a high-pitched voice.

Janitor Gary gave the parrot a fond look. "You know, I think the little fellow's really taken a liking to you."

Harvey gave a sickly grin, flinching as Percy shifted again on his shoulder.

Nevaeh took a bite of cookie, brushing nonexistent crumbs from her pristine white outfit.

"Percy wants a cookie!" the parrot squawked suddenly, making Harvey jump. *"Percy wants a cookie!"*

"For the last time, you're on a diet!" Janitor Gary snapped at the bird. "You know what the vet said!"

The bird made a rude noise, flapping its wings in annoyance.

Harvey picked a feather out of his hair, gingerly lifted his teacup, and took a sip of the brownish-gray liquid.

To his dismay, it also *tasted* like hot mushrooms mixed with feet.

"Mmm," he choked out, his eyes watering. "Delicious."

Janitor Gary sat back in his chair, beaming. "I'm so glad you like it," he told Harvey. "Believe it or not, I don't receive many visitors in the boiler room."

A loud hiss of scalding-hot steam blasted from the vent just above Harvey's shoulder, narrowly missing his head.

"Huh," Harvey said. "I can't imagine why."

"Anyway," Stella said, "like we said before, we were hoping we might ask you a few questions about the lost-and-found box? Specifically, about the curse?"

Janitor Gary sighed. "I always knew this day would come," he said. "But after all these years, I'd hoped . . ." He trailed off, pulling himself together with visible effort. "I assume you've already talked to Primrose?"

Stella nodded. "Briefly. She sort of . . . fled in terror when we tried to question her. But we found her scrapbook," she said, passing Coach Johnson's album over to Janitor Gary. "We saw the pictures of her and her friend Barty down in the basement. And we were wondering if you—"

"If *you* were the same Bartholomew Gary pictured in this photo," Nevaeh finished for her, pulling a folded piece of paper from her pocket and holding it up for Janitor Gary to see.

Stella gaped at her. "You *tore* a page out of the yearbook? What if Librarian Pat finds out?"

"Thief!" Percy squawked in indignation, bobbing his head excitedly. "Smuggler! *Brigand!*"

Nevaeh rolled her eyes.

"Ah. Now, this takes me back," Janitor Gary said, flipping eagerly through the pages of the scrapbook. "Primrose and I must have been about your age here. We were inseparable. Always laughing, getting into scrapes . . ." His smile fell as he came to the last pages of the album. "Until the basement, that is."

Stella pulled her notebook from her pocket. "What happened?" she asked. "Tell us everything!"

Janitor Gary shook his head. "We were young and foolish back then. Always poking our noses where they didn't belong. One day, Primrose and I decided to explore the basement. At first it was fun. But then we wandered off the beaten path." The janitor's eyes clouded at the memory. "The basement seemed to go on forever. It grew darker and darker and darker. We were hopelessly lost."

Harvey shivered, goose bumps rising on his arms.

"We wandered for hours," Janitor Gary went on. "It felt like *days*. Who knows how long we would have been lost if we hadn't found it?"

"*It?*" Stella questioned, her notebook at the ready.

"Why, the shipwreck, of course," Janitor Gary said, shrugging.

Stella's pencil paused mid-scratch. "I'm sorry, the *what?*"

The janitor leaned forward. "The *shipwreck*," he repeated, in a slightly louder voice. "An actual *pirate* ship, still perfectly preserved after all those years."

"Interesting," Nevaeh said, making a note in her own notebook. "Tell me, Janitor Gary, would you say you and Coach Johnson were suffering from the effects of dehydration at that time? Dizziness? Light-headedness? Confusion?"

Even Stella looked a little dubious. "A *pirate ship*?" she asked. "Are you . . . sure?"

"I don't understand," Harvey said. "How could a pirate ship end up in the basement? I mean, isn't Strangeville *landlocked*?"

"Primrose and I could hardly believe it either," Janitor Gary said. "It didn't feel real until we were standing inside."

"You went *inside* the ship?" Stella asked, leaning forward in her chair, her pencil poised expectantly over her notebook. "What did you find?"

"Let me guess," Harvey said, his stomach sinking. "A treasure chest."

Percy nipped at his ear.

"Exactly," Janitor Gary said, nodding. "Or, as *you* know it, the lost-and-found box."

"Of course," Stella muttered to herself, scribbling furiously. "It all makes sense."

Nevaeh narrowed her eyes. "But *does* it?" she asked. "Does it *really*?"

"The chest was locked," Janitor Gary went on. "But Primrose was strong, even as a child. She managed to break the lock with her bare hands. Inside, we found—"

"What?" Stella asked eagerly. "You found *what*?"

Nevaeh shot Stella a look of exasperation. "You know, if you'd stop interrupting, he could *tell* us!"

"It was . . . junk," Janitor Gary said, shrugging his shoulders. "We found *junk*. Spare shirts, half-burned candles, a frying pan or two . . . Primrose and I couldn't believe it."

Nevaeh lifted an eyebrow sardonically. "I guess one man's trash really *is* another one's treasure."

"Primrose and I didn't know what to do," Janitor Gary went on. "We were still hopelessly lost. We were hungry. We were thirsty. And, most importantly, we really, *really* had to go to the bathroom." He paused, shaking his head at the memory. "It was awful. Who *knows* what would have happened to us if I hadn't found the compass at the bottom of the chest?"

Harvey felt suddenly ill. "I'm sorry," he said, his voice a little unsteady. "Did you say . . . a *compass*?"

Janitor Gary nodded. "It felt like an omen. Like a sign. Like *fate*. We told ourselves no one would ever miss it. After all, it was just a dented old compass! Who would possibly care?"

Harvey privately wondered if he was about to vomit.

"Luckily, I'd taken a few orienteering courses," Janitor Gary went on. "I used the compass to find our way home. Primrose carried the chest with her on her back: a small souvenir to show our friends. Not that anyone believed us about the pirate ship anyway." He paused, shooting a fond look in the parrot's direction. "At the last minute, Percy swooped out of nowhere and joined us. The poor little blighter must have been down there all alone. Still guarding his captain's treasure, even after all those years."

Percy shook his feathers out, preening a little at the attention.

Nevaeh looked dubious. "You know, according to the scientific principle of Occam's razor, the simplest explanation is usually the best one," she said. "Are we sure the parrot didn't just . . . escape from a local pet store?"

Janitor Gary ignored her. "By the time Primrose

and I made it out of the basement, we were ready to forget the whole adventure. We left the chest in the cafeteria and went about our business. But it wasn't long before strange things began to happen around the school. *Piratey* things," he clarified. "Nothing serious, to begin with: a touch of scurvy here, a spot of dysentery there. Sea chanteys would get stuck in our heads for hours at a time."

"Like Arjun!" Stella whispered to Harvey and Nevaeh. "In gym class this morning!"

"Primrose and I didn't think much of it, at first. But then things started to escalate. . . ."

Harvey swallowed. "Escalate *how*?" he squeaked.

"The hallways flooded with salt water," the janitor said. "Sharks appeared out of nowhere, circling the classrooms for blood. And then the kraken appeared—"

Harvey blinked. "The *kraken*?" he repeated. "As in . . . the giant mythical sea beast? The legendary monster of the ocean? The colossal squid of the seven seas? *That* kind of kraken?"

"Oh good," Janitor Gary said, nodding in approval. "You've heard of it."

Nevaeh looked impatient. "Krakens aren't real," she said. "Everyone knows that."

"I assure you," Janitor Gary told her, his voice haunted, "krakens are *very* real indeed."

"What happened next?" Stella asked, her pencil momentarily stilling over her notebook.

A faraway look entered Janitor Gary's eyes. "I remember the screams most of all. The confusion. The *terror.*" He shook his head at the memory. "My hair went white almost instantly. The west wing of the school was destroyed within minutes. Hundreds were injured; dozens more were missing. And it was all our fault. Primrose and I had stolen the compass from the treasure chest. *We* had awakened the curse."

Harvey swallowed. Beneath his fingers, the compass felt red hot. "So, how did you stop it?" he asked. "How did you save the school?"

"Primrose and I knew we had to return the compass to its rightful owner," Janitor Gary replied, visibly gathering himself. "Primrose carried the chest. I carried the compass. And together, we ventured into the basement once more. Somehow, impossibly, we managed to find the shipwreck and return the compass to the treasure chest." He paused, looking shaken. "We barely made it out alive. The guilt at what we'd done was almost too much to bear; we could hardly stand to *look* at each other, let alone be friends."

The janitor paused again, clearing his throat.

"We thought it was the end of it. That the pirate's curse had been lifted. But then, one day, the treasure chest reappeared . . . ," Janitor Gary told the children. "We tried to warn our friends, but they wouldn't listen. To everyone else, the chest appeared to be a harmless lost-and-found box. People didn't seem to notice that things came back different. That things came back *wrong*."

The janitor drew a deep breath, straightening his shoulders. "Primrose and I made each other a vow. We promised to always stay at Strangeville. To watch over the chest. To make sure that no one *ever* triggered the curse again. And for *fifty years* we've kept that promise. But now, the curse is back. *The compass has been stolen once more.* And until it's returned, we're all in danger! We're all in *terrible dang—*"

The sound of a bell rang overhead, cutting Janitor Gary off mid-sentence.

"Oh dear!" the janitor said, jumping to his feet. "Is that the time? I should have been back at work six minutes ago!"

"Wait!" Stella said. "But the compass! The curse! The pirate ship! How do we find the ship?"

Janitor Gary was already halfway through the door, a large mop clutched in his hands. "Primrose and I made a map, in case we ever needed to find it again!" he called over his shoulder. "Just look behind B-seven! You can't miss it!"

"B-seven?" Stella repeated. "But what does that even—"

The door closed with a loud clang behind Janitor Gary, cutting Stella off mid-sentence.

"Well, that's just great," Stella said, flipping her notebook shut in annoyance. "What are we supposed to do now?"

There was a moment of silence, broken only by Percy's voice.

"Ahoy, mateys!" the bird squawked triumphantly. "Ye be doomed!"

18

An Announcement

Hello again, Strangeville! It's Vice President Capozzi here with a few *exciting* afternoon announcements for you all!

First off, I'm pleased to announce that Chef Louis has recovered his lost finger! Nurse Porter has already successfully reattached the digit, which, aside from a few teeth marks, is no worse for the wear!

Congratulations to Chef Louis, and let's all give Nurse Porter a big hand!

Although perhaps not quite so literally, next time . . .

In other news, sixth grader Belinda Boogerton has just returned from a family vacation to the Corn Palace of Mitchell, South Dakota! Belinda has *several* photo albums of the trip that she would like to share with any interested students, as well as a fourteen-hour slideshow commemorating the event. Belinda has also written a one-woman amateur theater performance about the experience!

Sounds wonderful, Belinda!

What a shame that I'm allergic to monologues . . .

Finally, I'm sorry to say that rumors of a certain "curse" continue to plague the hallways of Strangeville School, despite absolutely *no* evidence of such a thing! I can assure you there's absolutely *nothing* sinister about our beloved lost-and-found box! And I'm *certainly* not just saying that in a desperate attempt to mask my own fear!

Ha-ha-ha-ha-ha-ha!

Ahem.

Yes.

Anyway, this is Vice Principal Capozzi, signing off! Hopefully not forever . . .

Science Class

"Well," Harvey said, settling into his seat in the science room. "On the plus side, we *did* figure out how Janitor Gary's hair went white."

Percy bobbed back and forth on Harvey's shoulder, looking interestedly around the room.

"Seriously?" Stella asked, sitting down next to Harvey. "*That's* the information you're choosing to focus on?"

"Sorry," Harvey said. "Sometimes I joke under stress. My mom says it's a coping mechanism."

Stella rolled her eyes. "Try to concentrate, would you? The fate of the entire school is in our hands."

She pulled out her notebook and flipped through the pages. "*Someone* must have taken the compass from the lost-and-found box. We just need to figure out *who.*"

Guilt flooded through Harvey.

For *fifty* years, Coach Johnson and Janitor Gary had managed to keep the curse of the lost-and-found box at bay.

And then Harvey had come along and ruined everything.

What had he been thinking, taking the compass?

Harvey wasn't like his grandfather.

He wasn't *brave.* He wasn't *daring.* He wasn't an *adventurer.*

Harvey didn't even know how to *use* a compass.

Did you just . . . *point it* in the direction you wanted to go?

Did that even make *sense?*

Did *anything* make sense anymore?

(Harvey had a lot of questions. He was also using a *lot* of italics!)

"What about the treasure map?" he asked, changing the subject. "Janitor Gary said we had to 'look behind B-seven,' remember?"

"Oh, come on," Nevaeh said, turning around

from her table and looking between Harvey and Stella. "Don't tell me you actually *believed* him. I mean, pirate ships? Treasure chests? A *kraken*?"

Harvey shivered.

Percy dug his claws into Harvey's shoulder, flapping his wings for balance.

"Of course I believed him," Stella said. "Did you forget about the race car? Or the robot? Or the fact that Arjun burst into a *sea chantey* in the middle of gym class?" She shook her head, looking worried. "The curse is definitely escalating. We need to figure out how to stop it before things get *really* bad."

Harvey nodded. "Agreed."

He promised himself to return the compass to the cafeteria as soon as he could slip away unnoticed. Hopefully, it wouldn't be too late.

Nevaeh threw her hands up in the air. "Is *everyone* at this school delusional?"

Stella shrugged. "This is Strangeville," she told Nevaeh. "What did you expect?"

"Goggles on, class!" Ms. Crumbleton called from the front of the room. "Remember: when it comes to science, safety first!"

Harvey looked down at the collection of glass

vials sitting on the table in front of him and Stella. Noxious smoke coiled from the tops of several of them while liquids bubbled ominously in others.

He edged his chair a few inches away from the table.

Arjun raised his hand. "I thought breakfast came first."

"No, it's family," Evie corrected him. "Family comes first; breakfast comes second."

"*Lunch* comes second," Nicolas said confidently. "Safety is third."

"Don't forget your gloves!" Ms. Crumbleton called, tugging a rubber glove over her hand with a loud snap. "And remember, as long as you follow the instructions exactly, this experiment is *perfectly* safe!"

One of the vials in front of Harvey gave a sucking belch, spitting purplish liquid onto the table in front of him. With a soft hiss, the liquid ate through the wood, narrowly missing the tips of Harvey's shoes as it dripped to the floor below.

Harvey edged his chair a few more inches away from the table.

Stella didn't even blink.

"B-seven could be a bingo number," she told Harvey. "Or an airplane. Or a guitar chord? Ooh, or a vitamin!"

Another bubble of liquid belched from the top of the nearest test tube and grazed the side of Harvey's head as it went past.

The air filled with the smell of burnt hair.

Harvey decided to ignore it. "How could Janitor Gary hide a treasure map behind a *vitamin*?" he asked.

At the front of the room, Ms. Crumbleton stepped into a white Teflon hazmat suit and zipped the front securely. "Don't forget your goggles, people!" she called, slipping a pair over her head. "This is how you lose an eye!"

"Well, it's got to be *something*," Stella said. "*Think*. Where would someone hide something if they wanted to make sure no one *ever* found it?"

At the table next to them, Nevaeh suddenly stiffened.

For a moment, Harvey was worried that she had accidentally inhaled some of the noxious gas.

But then Nevaeh's hand shot up in the air. "Ms. Crumbleton?"

"Yes, Nevaeh?" the science teacher asked. "Do you have a question about the experiment?"

"Actually, I was wondering if Stella and Harvey and I could have a hall pass?" Nevaeh asked. "We all have to use the bathroom."

Stella looked at her in confusion. "We do?"

Nevaeh turned, giving Stella a warning look. "Yes," she said meaningfully. "We do."

"Well, hurry back," Ms. Crumbleton said, lowering her face shield. "You don't want to miss all the fun!"

Nevaeh stood up, gathering her things together. "Come on," she whispered to Harvey and Stella. "*I know where the map is.*"

The Treasure Map

"Say you need to hide something important," Nevaeh said, leading the way down the hallway. "Something secret. Something *special.* Logically speaking, you'd want to pick the *very* last place someone would ever look, wouldn't you?"

"But I thought you didn't even *believe* in the curse," Stella said, hurrying to keep up with Nevaeh's longer legs.

"I don't!" Nevaeh called over her shoulder. "But Janitor Gary *does*! Which means he and Coach Johnson definitely hid *something*."

She pushed opened the door to the teachers' lounge and strode confidently through the room. Harvey and Stella followed more cautiously, sticking their heads inside first to make sure there weren't any teachers lurking nearby.

On the other side of the room, Nevaeh had come to a stop. "If you think about it, there's only one rational hiding place," she said. "A place so vile, so disgusting, so *unbelievably horrifying* that no one would *ever* stumble across it, not even by accident." She gestured proudly in front of herself. *"The teachers' lounge vending machine."*

Stella and Harvey both gaped up at the vending machine. Behind the machine's glass front sat row after row of repulsive-looking snacks, each one neatly labeled with a specific letter and number.

"'A-one,'" Stella read aloud. "'Boiled turnip blasters.'"

Harvey's stomach lurched.

"'D-eight,'" Harvey read. "'Pre-moistened Tofurky jerky.'"

His stomach lurched again.

"'B-seven,'" Nevaeh said, tapping her finger against the glass. "'Curdled milk lumps, extra spicy.'"

Harvey's stomach attempted to climb out of his windpipe and escape.

"And look what's behind it," Nevaeh said, a note of triumph in her voice. A large sheet of paper was folded tightly into a rectangle, wedged just behind the bag of curdled milk lumps.

Next to Harvey, Stella stiffened. "The map," she whispered. *You found the map.*

"Wait a minute," Harvey said, catching sight of the price tag beneath. "*Six dollars* for curdled milk lumps?"

"It's actually a pretty good price," Nevaeh told him. "You'd pay double that in a movie theater."

Harvey shook his head. "I don't understand how this place keeps getting weirder."

Nevaeh reached into the pocket of her skirt and pulled out a credit card. "Don't worry about paying me back," she told Harvey. "I have an expense account with NASA." She inserted the credit card into the slot and punched the buttons for B-7.

The disused machine whirred dustily to life. There was a pause, and then the curdled milk lumps edged forward, and finally fell to the plastic tray with a wet thud.

Harvey shuddered.

Nevaeh punched B-7 into the machine again and waited impatiently for the map to fall. She pulled it from the plastic tray and unfolded the length of paper in front of her.

Harvey crowded next to her, peering down at the map.

It was drawn in pencil: an endless maze of twists and turns, full of looping detours and dead-end corridors. Ominous notes were scribbled across the map, things like HERE THERE BE WOLVES! and DON'T FORGET TO DUCK! and BEWARE OF FLUFFY!

"Fluffy?" Harvey asked nervously. "Who's Fluffy?"

"Look," Nevaeh said. "Here!" She pointed toward the far corner of the map, where a small, red *X* had been drawn in marker.

"Stella, look!" Harvey said. "*X* really *does* mark the . . ."

His voice trailed off as he realized his friend wasn't standing next to them anymore. In fact, she was nowhere to be seen.

"Stella?" Harvey said, his voice tight with worry. He turned to Nevaeh. "She's *gone!*"

The Lost-and-Found
Box (Again)

"Don't worry," Stella said, her voice drifting list-lessly through the air. "I'm right here."

Harvey rushed forward to peer over the edge of the couch. Stella was lying full-length across the cushions, her head resting against a particularly lumpy throw pillow.

"Stella! Are you okay?" Harvey asked worriedly. "What's wrong?"

He made his way around the couch and wedged himself awkwardly beneath Stella's feet. After a moment, Nevaeh hesitatingly made her way over as well, and perched on the edge of a nearby armchair. She smoothed the map over her knee, the page crinkling loudly.

"I'm fine," Stella said, shaking her head. "It's silly. I just . . ." She paused, glancing in Nevaeh's direction. "I guess I thought *I* would be the one to find the map," she said, in a small voice. "I mean, it's *my* story. *I'm* the lead reporter for the *Strangeville School Gazette*. No offense, Nevaeh, but you don't even *believe* in the curse."

Nevaeh looked down at the map on her lap.

(Hey, that rhymes!)

For a moment, there was only silence.

And then Nevaeh looked up. "Do you know what it's like to have everyone just *assume* that you'll win a Nobel Prize by the time you're fourteen?" she asked.

Harvey and Stella glanced at each other.

"Er . . . no?" Harvey admitted.

"I've been working for NASA since I was seven years old," Nevaeh went on. "It hasn't always been easy." She paused, straightening her shoulders. "I realized early on that if I wanted people to take me seriously, I had to become a *serious* person. So I did."

Nevaeh looked down, picking at the edge of the map.

"I guess I just wanted to be . . . someone *different* for a while. Someone *fun*. The kind of person who chases after *treasure maps* instead of chasing after spare rocket-part reimbursement receipts." She looked up at Harvey and Stella. "Does that make sense?"

Harvey felt the compass in his pocket, his fingers clenching the metal tightly. "Trust me," he said, swallowing the lump in his throat. "I know *all* about wanting to be someone else."

"Well, for what it's worth, if you ever decide to take a break from NASA, I think you'd make a really good reporter," Stella told Nevaeh.

Nevaeh smiled. "Thanks," she said. "But I think I'll leave the journalism to you." She wrinkled her nose. "Is it just me, or do numbers make *way* more sense than people?"

"Who knows?" Stella asked glumly. "With the way this investigation is going, maybe *I'll* end up becoming a rocket scientist too."

Nevaeh stood up, planting her hands firmly on her hips. "Don't be ridiculous," she said. "You're a *great* reporter. Who found all those missing ferrets in the fall? Who exposed the truth behind Chef Louis's mystery macaroni? Who uncovered the greatest toilet-paper scandal this school has ever seen? *You* did."

Harvey turned to Stella, raising his eyebrows. "There was a toilet-paper scandal?" he asked.

Stella blushed, giving a modest wave of her hand. "I had to go undercover as a used-toilet-paper salesperson to get the story," she told Harvey. "It took three weeks, but it was worth it."

Harvey blinked. "Did you say a '*used*-toilet-paper salesperson'?"

"You're right," Stella told Nevaeh, bouncing to her feet. "I *am* a great reporter. I think I just . . . get a little *too* competitive, sometimes. You know?"

"I may have gotten carried away as well," Nevaeh admitted. "What do you say we forget about the bet?"

"Deal." Stella stuck out her hand, offering it to Nevaeh. "As long as you agree to help us end this curse once and for all, that is."

Nevaeh shook Stella's hand. "Deal," she said. "Even though, you know . . . curses aren't real."

Stella grinned.

"Come on," she told Harvey and Nevaeh. "Let's get out of here before someone catches us."

"Good plan," Harvey said, hurrying toward the door. He pulled it open and blinked in surprise as ice-cold water poured across his feet.

"Well," he said, peering at the hallway. Which was now, troublingly, completely underwater. "That's new."

22

An Announcement

Good afternoon, students! This is Vice Principal Capozzi here with some important seventh-period announcements.

In unfortunate news, a page has just been discovered missing in a library copy of the 1974 edition of the *Strangeville School Yearbook*. Librarian Pat is, of course, *devastated* and has vowed to hunt down the perpetrators of this heinous act with all possible speed. Librarian Pat tells me he will "not eat, nor sleep, *nor* change his underwear" until the page has been returned.

Remember, Strangeville, not all heroes wear capes!

Although most of them *do* wear fresh underwear. . . .

Moving on, I'm sorry to announce that the smell of delicious baked goods wafting from the East Hallway has lured the wolves from their dark basement den. On the plus side, the French club and the German club have finally united in the face of a common enemy! On the minus side, several members of each club have been bitten by wolves.

The injured students have already been transferred to the nurse's office and are currently under the knowledgeable care of our very own Nurse Porter!

While all involved parties are expected to make a full recovery, Nurse Porter informs me that she *is* "running low on leeches" and, quote, "even lower on patience."

In summary, students should *avoid* being bitten by wolves if possible.

And, last but not least, Strangeville, I've just been informed that the West Hallway is currently underwater! No need for alarm! In fact, are we sure that the West Hallway hasn't *always* been underwater?

Lifeguards are already on hand to distribute safety vests and swim floaties to all students passing through the hallway. The buddy system *is* recommended, as several shark sightings have been reported in the area.

Students are reminded to wait at least *thirty* minutes after eating before swimming with the sharks. Again, under *no* circumstances should you swim with the sharks directly after lunch, or you *could* develop a dangerous cramp in your stomach.

This is Vice Principal Capozzi signing off, for now.

And remember, Strangeville: a shark bite is just a hug with teeth!

An Unexpected Problem

The delicious smell of fish fingers still lingered in the cafeteria.

Nevaeh poked her head into the room, looking cautiously around before signaling for Harvey and Stella to follow her inside. The tables had been cleared already, covered with snowy white tablecloths, and laid with fresh silverware for tomorrow. Luckily, the maître d' was nowhere to be seen.

"Wait up," Harvey whispered, following Nevaeh and Stella through the maze of empty tables. His shoes squelched loudly with every step, leaving a trail of puddles in his wake.

Percy angled his head to the side, sniffing the fragrant air.

"Time for yum-yums!" the bird croaked loudly. "Percy wants a cracker!"

"No crackers," Harvey said firmly. "You *know* you're on a diet."

Percy bit his ear.

"Ouch!" Harvey yelped, stumbling over one of his sodden shoes.

"Shh," Nevaeh scolded them.

Percy stuck his tongue out at her.

(Yes, parrots have tongues. It's a fact. Look it up.)

With Harvey still rubbing his sore earlobe, they rounded the last table and came wordlessly to a stop in front of the lost-and-found box.

Or, rather, where the lost-and-found box used to be.

"It's *gone,*" Stella said, poking the patch of bare carpet with her foot. "Somebody must have taken it."

"What do we do now?" Harvey asked, panic beginning to set in. The brass compass was a millstone in his pocket, growing heavier with every second.

Harvey felt as though he might sink right through the floor with the weight of his guilt. "How are we supposed to fix the curse of the lost-and-found box if we can't even *find* the lost-and-found box?"

"Maybe we should check the basement," Stella said. "We're running out of time. The hallways are already flooding. What if the kraken appears?"

"Again," Nevaeh said, "krakens don't exist. But I *might* be able to help find the box."

"Really?" Stella and Harvey asked in unison. "How?"

Nevaeh pointed toward the floor. "Look at the carpet," she said. "It's glowing."

Harvey squinted down at the floor.

To his surprise, the carpet *was* glowing: a faint, greenish shimmer roughly the shape of a rectangle.

Or a treasure chest.

"The box must have rubbed off on the carpet somehow," Stella said.

"How?" Harvey asked. "Like . . . *magically?*"

"I'm sure there's a perfectly logical scientific explanation for it," Nevaeh said. "Some sort of bioluminescent powder, maybe. Or a dinoflagellate of some sort."

What's a dinoflagellate? Harvey mouthed to Stella.

Stella shrugged.

Dinoflagellates, as most people know, are a common type of single-cell plankton, many of which are bioluminescent, or able to glow in the dark.

Often referred to as a type of algae, dinoflagellates live in both salt water and fresh water and have two whiplike tails known as flagella. Some dinoflagellates have a symbiotic, or mutually helpful, relationship with marine invertebrates such as jellyfish and coral. But dinoflagellates can also produce a poison that builds up in the bodies of shellfish. Eating those shellfish can lead to poisoning in people and other animals.

The word *dinoflagellate* spelled backward is *etallegalfonid.*

But, anyway.

Enough about dinoflagellates!

Let's get back to Harvey.

"Come on," Nevaeh told him, motioning for Harvey to help. "Let's just get a sample of the carpet back to my laboratory."

Stella gaped at her. "Wait. You have a *laboratory?*"

Nevaeh broke into a grin.

"Oh yeah," she said. "I *definitely* have a laboratory."

Nevaeh's Laboratory

"Whoa," Harvey said, peering around the enormous room in awe. "This place is unbelievable. It looks like a spaceship. Only . . . *cleaner!*"

Nevaeh's laboratory was gleaming white, filled with complicated, blinking machinery and sleek chrome countertops. Everywhere Harvey looked there were beakers, and test tubes, and Bunsen burners, and flasks, and things he didn't even know the names of.

There was a low, ever-present hum in the background, as if the entire room could *lift off* at any moment.

"This place is amazing," Stella said, spinning around in a slow circle. "Why have I never been in here before? In fact, why have I never even *heard* about this place?"

"Because I'm the only one with a key," Nevaeh said, her voice matter-of-fact. "Even Vice Principal Capozzi isn't allowed in here." She pulled a spotless white lab coat from its peg on the wall and slipped her arms into the sleeves.

It fit her perfectly.

"Bring the carpet sample over to the chemical spectrometer," Nevaeh told Harvey, pulling a pair of protective goggles over her head. Miraculously, she managed to do so without moving a single hair out of place. "I want to get some initial readouts on its composition."

"Right," Harvey said, looking around the room. "Er . . . which one is the chemical spectrometer again?"

"Here," Nevaeh said, taking the sample from him. "Let me do it."

Harvey gladly handed it over to her, then wiped his sweaty palms against his jeans. As Nevaeh calmly set to work, he and Stella wandered around the laboratory, taking everything in.

Harvey paused in front of a framed photo on one of the counters. It showed Nevaeh posed next to a chubby animal with brown fur, stubby legs, and adorably squashed cheeks. "Aw," he said. "Is this your dog?"

"Mangy mutt!" Percy squawked, bristling his feathers. *"Mangy mutt!"*

"It's a wombat," Nevaeh said briskly, without looking up from her work. "And it's not a pet; it's a wild animal. I'm fostering it for the local wombat rehabilitation shelter."

Harvey peered more closely at the photo. "If it's not a pet, why is it wearing a tiny little bow tie?" he asked.

Nevaeh pretended not to hear him.

"What does this do?" Stella asked, stopping in front of a small rectangular machine covered in strange buttons and dials. "It looks like a microwave."

"It's an oscilloscope," Nevaeh said absently, fiddling with the spectrometer's controls. "It displays voltage signals as waveforms, then plots them on a graph, showing a visual representation of voltage variation over time."

"Cool," Harvey said, joining Stella in front of the

machine. He reached out to poke experimentally at one of the buttons.

"Do you mind?" Nevaeh asked, glancing up from the spectrometer. "I have everything calibrated to my specific specifications. Plus, there's a one-in-seven chance that you'll accidentally blow us all up."

"Shiver me timbers!" Percy squawked. *"Shiver me timbers!"*

Harvey and Stella quickly backed away from the machine.

"Got it," Harvey said. "We'll just . . . stand here. In the middle of the room. Not touching anything."

"That would probably be for the best," Nevaeh agreed, lowering her head again.

Several long moments passed in silence, broken only by the quiet beep of Nevaeh's machinery.

Nevaeh finished her spectrometer testing and moved on to the microarray fluorescence and colorimetric plate scanner.

Harvey scratched his nose.

Nevaeh scanned the carpet sample with the infrared moisture analyzer, searching for any anomalies.

Stella scratched her ear.

Nevaeh ran a sample through the Q700 sonicator, using the sound waves to agitate the particles into a liquid solution.

Harvey scratched his butt.

Finally, after what seemed like a million years but was probably closer to five minutes, Nevaeh looked up from her research. "Interesting," she said aloud. "Very interesting."

"What is it?" Harvey asked eagerly. "Did you find something?"

"Is there a way to track down the lost-and-found box?" Stella added.

"You tell me," Nevaeh said, stepping aside from the microscope she was using and gesturing for them to join her.

Harvey and Stella hurried across the lab and took turns peering down into the microscope. Tiny bright-green particles drifted slowly back and forth, suspended in the drop of water Nevaeh had placed on the glass slide. To Harvey, it looked like a miniature night sky, glowing with the light of a thousand stars.

"Er, what exactly are we looking at?" he asked, standing up from the microscope.

"As I suspected," Nevaeh said, "the glow is coming from bioluminescent dinoflagellates. They're producing light using a typical luciferin-luciferase reaction."

Harvey and Stella stared at her blankly.

"Luciferase is an enzyme," Nevaeh explained. "It interacts with oxidized luciferin to create oxyluciferin, which generates light."

Harvey and Stella stared at her blankly some more.

Nevaeh sighed. "Algae," she told them. "Glow-in-the-dark algae."

"Ohhhh," Harvey and Stella said together.

"Nincompoops!" Percy squawked. "Glow-in-the dark *nincompoops!*"

"You're the nincompoop!" Stella told the parrot. "And that makes sense," she added, turning to Nevaeh. "Algae grow in the ocean, right? So that means the lost-and-found box really *is* from a pirate ship."

"Not necessarily," Nevaeh told her. "Algae grow *everywhere,* not just the ocean. For all we know, the lost-and-found box came from *Iowa.*"

"So, wait," Harvey said. "How do the algae help us find the box, then?"

"They don't," Nevaeh said.

His face fell.

"Which is why I ran the sample *again*," Nevaeh said with a grin. "The particles are emitting a surprising amount of gamma rays, as well as several other elements that I've never seen before."

Harvey glared at Stella. "I *told* you it was radioactive!"

"I'm sure it's fine," Stella said. "Right, Nevaeh?"

"Here," Nevaeh told her, neatly sidestepping the question. She rummaged in one of the cabinets, then pulled down a boxy yellow device roughly the shape of a toaster. "It's a Geiger counter. If I'm right, it should lead us straight to the lost-and-found box."

She flicked the switch on.

Nothing happened.

"Huh," Nevaeh said. "That's weird."

She flicked it off, then on again.

Still nothing.

Nevaeh frowned. "It must be out of batteries."

Stella gave a long-suffering sigh. "Of course it is." She pulled her backpack off her shoulder and unzipped the top. Inside the bag, Harvey glimpsed a carton of dental floss, six bottles of Elmer's glue, and a signed VHS copy of Richard Simmons's *Sweatin' to the Oldies* workout tape.

"So, what are we talking about here?" Stella asked Nevaeh. "Double A? Triple A? *Quadruple* A?"

"It's an anodized 4R25 zinc-carbon dry-cell battery," Nevaeh said. "Extra large."

"Seriously?" Harvey said, as Stella began to rummage around in her backpack. "Who would carry something like that around with—"

"Got it!" Stella interrupted, handing Nevaeh the massive battery.

"Of course you do," Harvey said, shaking his head.

Nevaeh slotted the battery neatly into the back of the Geiger counter.

With a loud burst of static, it clicked to life.

"Cool," Stella said, peering at the bright yellow machine. "So, how does it work?"

"We just need to follow the spikes in gamma-ray activity," Nevaeh told them. "It's so easy, a *child* could do it."

"We *are* children," Stella told her.

"Then we won't have any problems!" Nevaeh said brightly.

"Trust me," Harvey said darkly. "We *always* have problems."

"Don't be such a worrywart," Stella told Harvey. "Now come on. Let's go save the school!"

The Tentacle

"I have a bad feeling about this," Harvey said, peering down at the Geiger counter in Nevaeh's hands. The machine was making a strange clicking noise, its needle fluctuating wildly on the display.

"You have a bad feeling about *everything*," Stella said.

"That's not true," Harvey insisted. "I just have a bad feeling about *most* things."

Nevaeh set off at a brisk pace, sweeping the Geiger counter from side to side in front of her.

"I wonder what class we're supposed to be in

right now," Harvey commented, peering uneasily around the empty hallway.

Stella shrugged. "I wouldn't worry about it," she said. "Thomas Edison didn't go to school, and look what happened to him!"

"I guess," Harvey said. "Wait, wasn't he the one who was struck by lightning?"

"That was Benjamin Franklin," Stella said. "Thomas Edison invented the telephone."

"Alexander Graham Bell invented the telephone," Nevaeh corrected her. "Well, with the help of Lewis Latimer, anyway. Thomas Edison invented the *light bulb.*" She shook her head. "You guys *really* need to go to class more often."

Nevaeh was just rounding the corner when she smacked headfirst into a tall, nervous-looking man wearing a corduroy suit and a worried expression.

In what can only be described as a three-car-pileup situation, Stella smacked into Nevaeh. Harvey, rounding the corner after her, smacked into both of them.

Percy gave a squawk of alarm, digging his claws into Harvey's shoulder for balance.

"Vice Principal Capozzi?" Stella asked, shaking

her head a little dazedly. Her ponytail whipped Harvey in the face, making him sputter. "What are you doing here?"

The vice principal straightened his corduroy vest, peering down at the children. "I could ask you the same thing, Ms. Cho," he said. "I assume you all have hall passes?"

Harvey gave a nervous gulp.

"We're actually looking for the lost-and-found box," Stella said. "You haven't seen it, have you? It's gone missing from the cafeteria."

Vice Principal Capozzi's face blanched. "Oh dear," he said. "The lost-and-found box is gone *already*?" He straightened his corduroy tie. "That *does* complicate matters, doesn't it?"

"Complicate matters how?" Nevaeh asked curiously.

The vice principal glanced quickly around the hallway, making sure they were alone. "Yes. Er, well, as it turns out," he said, lowering his voice to a conspiratorial whisper, "there may be *some* truth to these rumors of a 'curse' after all."

Harvey rubbed his sore elbow, remembering how he'd narrowly escaped Evie's out-of-control race car. He was fairly certain the car's eerie green headlights would haunt his nightmares for the next few weeks.

Or the next few years.

"But don't worry, children!" Vice Principal Capozzi said, adopting a hearty tone. "I'm sure it will all be fine! After all, how bad can a kraken or two really be?"

Nevaeh opened her mouth to inform the vice principal that krakens weren't real.

But before she could say a word, the floor gave a sudden lurch. It rippled beneath them, heaving up and down with a tremendous cracking noise. It was almost as if some giant, unseen creature was passing beneath them.

A creature like, say . . . a kraken, perhaps.

"Oh, I don't know," Stella said, as screams of terror floated out from beneath the bottom of the door of the nearest classroom. "I'm guessing . . . *pretty bad?*"

The door flew open, students fleeing the room in a panicked mass of pointy elbows and stomping feet.

"Single file, children!" their teacher called,

pausing to push the door shut behind him. "No need to panic! Everything is under control!"

A tentacle snaked its way through the door, wrapped itself around Mr. Ndiaye's leg, and yanked him off his feet. The tentacle was enormous, pinkish red in color, and covered on one side in huge yellow suckers.

The tentacle gave a thick, sucking shudder, wrapping itself more tightly around the teacher's leg. It began to pull him slowly back into the room.

"Oh dear," Mr. Ndiaye said, calmly contemplating the tentacle. "It appears things may be *slightly* less under control than I thought."

"Mr. Ndiaye!" Harvey yelled, diving for his math teacher.

Mr. Ndiaye was no stranger to danger, of course. Just last

month he had lost several toes during a *small* incident with a baby crocodile.

(It was fine. Mr. Ndiaye had always thought toes were slightly overrated.)

Percy abandoned ship, launching himself off Harvey's shoulder to land on the vice principal's head instead.

Harvey managed to fasten his arms around Mr. Ndiaye's waist, and he yanked backward as the huge, slimy tentacle pulled inexorably in the other direction.

Stella and Nevaeh quickly ran forward to help Harvey.

Loose change tumbled from Mr. Ndiaye's pockets as the tentacle tossed him wildly through the air, the children lurching below.

"Pop quiz, children!" the math teacher called, pointing at the floor. "If a large, tentacled sea beast shakes loose three quarters, five dimes, seven nickels, and eleven pennies from my pocket, how much spare change have I lost?"

"Pull!" Stella shouted, ignoring Mr. Ndiaye's question. She aimed a kick in the tentacle's direction, and the sole of her shoe connected with a loud squelch.

Oddly enough, it sounded *exactly* like a piece of wet celery slapping against a couch cushion.

"Heave, ho!" Percy squawked encouragingly in the background, still clinging to the vice principal's hair. *"Heave, ho!"*

Stella kicked again and again and again, her foot squelching with every blow. At last, the tentacle loosened just enough for them to yank Mr. Ndiaye free.

As they watched in relief, the tentacle slithered out of sight, leaving a trail of thick goo in its wake.

Thinking quickly, Harvey scrambled forward and slammed the door shut behind it.

Nevaeh stood up, offering the math teacher

a hand. "Are you okay, Mr. Ndiaye?" she asked. "Should we take you to see Nurse Porter?"

At the mention of the school nurse, Mr. Ndiaye grew pale. "No, no, I'm fine," he insisted, climbing hastily to his feet. "In fact, I've never been better!"

Stella looked down at her goo-coated foot. "Well, *I've* been better," she said. "These were my favorite shoes!"

Nevaeh shook her head, peering thoughtfully at the classroom door. "Interesting," she said. "I've never seen a squid *quite* that shade of pink before."

Stella grabbed the Geiger counter from the floor. "Come on," she told Harvey and Nevaeh. "We need to keep moving. Who knows how long we have before that thing attacks again?"

Harvey reluctantly stood up, and Percy fluttered back to his shoulder. "Fine," he said. "But only because *that* thing is leading us in the opposite direction," he added, nodding toward the Geiger counter.

"I suppose it could have been an octopus," Nevaeh murmured to herself, trailing absently after Stella and Harvey as they headed down the hallway. "Or an undiscovered species of cuttlefish, maybe?"

"Oh, please. How much more proof do you need?"

Stella said. "It was a *kraken*! My foot is *literally* covered in *kraken juice* right now!"

"But it *can't* be a kraken," Nevaeh argued, following her around the corner. "Krakens don't exist."

Left behind in the hallway, Mr. Ndiaye and Vice Principal Capozzi watched the children disappear around the corner, still arguing among themselves.

"You know, it's strange," Vice Principal Capozzi said, "but I can't help feeling like we should be *doing* something."

Mr. Ndiaye clapped him on the shoulder. "I wouldn't worry about it," he said comfortingly. "In my experience, these things tend to take care of themselves."

And, whistling a jaunty little tune, he strolled away.

26

An Announcement

Good afternoon, Strangeville. This is Vice Principal Capozzi checking in to say, *"Abandon ship!"*

27

The Return
of Coach Johnson

S tella trotted briskly up the stairwell, swish-
ing the Geiger counter in front of her. Her goo-
covered shoe squelched uncomfortably with
every step, but Stella refused to let it slow her
down.

Behind her, Nevaeh was still arguing with herself about cephalopods, struggling in vain to find a
logical explanation for the enormous, tentacled sea
beast currently lurking somewhere beneath the
math classroom.

Harvey caught the occasional muttered phrase,
like "Coleoidea subclass" or "chromatophore pig-

ment cells" or "Pull it together, Nevaeh! It was just a *tentacle!*"

The Geiger counter's clicking grew faster the higher they climbed, a rapid *tick-tick-tick-tick-tick* that matched the frantic beating of Harvey's heart.

How on earth had his grandfather managed to scale the highest peak of Mount Everest? Harvey could barely manage a flight of stairs without getting altitude sickness.

Harvey was also prone to various types of motion sickness, including but not limited to carsickness, airsickness, seasickness, trainsickness, and blimpsickness.

(Try saying *that* three times fast!)

"Er, could we maybe slow down a little bit?" he asked hopefully, trying to ignore the stitch in his side.

"No," Stella called over her shoulder. "We couldn't."

Harvey sighed. "I thought you might say that."

Percy gave Harvey's ear an encouraging nip. "Up and at 'em!" the parrot squawked. *"Up and at 'em!"*

They'd just reached the fifth-floor landing when the Geiger counter suddenly kicked into overdrive. *TICK-TICK-TICK-TICK-TICK* went the sensor, the needle flashing so quickly that Harvey felt dizzy.

"We're close," Stella breathed.

Harvey fought the urge to run.

Nevaeh stepped forward, taking the Geiger counter from Stella and sweeping it slowly back and forth.

"Here," she said, stopping in front of a closed classroom door. "It's in *here.*"

A dull thud echoed from the other side of the door.

Harvey blinked. "What was that?" he asked.

Another thud came from the depths of the classroom.

Stella took a deep breath. "Only one way to find out, I suppose," she said. "Everyone ready?"

Harvey frantically shook his head.

"Great," Stella said. "Let's go!"

And before Harvey could protest, she pulled the door open and barged into the classroom. Nevaeh followed closely behind, with Harvey reluctantly bringing up the rear.

From the far side of the room, Coach Johnson looked up in surprise, a massive axe suspended mid-swing above her head.

Glowing dimly on the floor in front of her was the lost-and-found box.

"Coach Johnson!" Stella shouted. "What are you doing? Stop!"

"You're too late!" the gym teacher cackled, a hysterical edge to her voice. She swung the enormous axe through the air, aiming the blow straight for the lost-and-found box. "The curse ends *now*!"

Harvey braced himself, waiting for the crashing splinter of metal against wood.

But instead there came another hollow thud.

As Harvey and the others watched in surprise, the axe glanced off the wooden chest without making a scratch, bouncing uselessly against the surface; it was almost as if there was some sort of force field surrounding the chest, protecting it from Coach Johnson's powerful blow.

For a moment, the children stood frozen, staring in shock.

And Percy fluttered into action.

"Batten down the hatches!" the bird squawked,

launching himself enthusiastically off Harvey's shoulder. *"It's a mutiny!"*

The bright red-and-yellow parrot zoomed through the air like a feathery, heat-seeking missile, aiming straight for Coach Johnson's head. "Percy, no!" Harvey shouted, but the parrot was already tangling his claws in the gym teacher's hair, tugging angrily at the roots.

Coach Johnson gave a shriek of alarm, dropping the axe to swat uselessly at Percy. "Get it off!" she shrieked. *"Get it off!"*

"Percy, *stop that!*" Harvey said desperately, rushing forward. "Bad parrot! *Bad!*"

Percy made a rude noise in his direction, yanking at another clump of Coach Johnson's hair.

After several attempts, Harvey finally managed to grab the parrot in midair. He tucked Percy's feathery little body into his armpit, cradling the bird like a football.

"I'm so sorry," he apologized to the gym teacher. "It's not his fault! He isn't housebroken yet."

Percy nipped at Harvey's armpit.

It was extremely painful.

"I never *did* like that bird," Coach Johnson murmured, casting a dirty look in the parrot's direction. "Why Barty wanted to keep the mangy macaw, I'll never know."

"For the last time," came a voice from behind them, "Percy *isn't* a macaw."

Coach Johnson and the children turned in surprise. Janitor Gary stood silhouetted against the door frame, his white hair glowing in the overhead light.

"Barty?" Coach Johnson asked, a small hitch in her voice. "After all this time . . . is it really *you*?"

"Hello, Primrose," Janitor Gary said, his voice thick with emotion. "You haven't changed a bit."

Nevaeh peered between the two adults, her forehead wrinkled in confusion. "You do realize that you work together, right?" she asked. "I mean, you *literally* see each other every day in the hallways."

"Shh!" Stella said, giving Nevaeh a stern look. "Let them talk!"

"We've failed, Barty," Coach Johnson whispered. "After all these years, it's happening *again*. Someone has stolen the compass. The curse has *returned!*"

"I know, Primrose," Janitor Gary said. He took a cautious step into the room. "I *know*. But destroying the chest won't end the curse. *We need to return the pirate's stolen treasure!*"

Coach Johnson's face turned gray. "I can't go back to the basement," she whispered. "I *won't!*"

"But *we* can!" Stella chimed in, her voice eager. She scrabbled in her backpack and pulled out a faded sheet of paper. "Look! We have your map! We can return the lost-and-found box to its rightful place! We can end the curse!"

"I know you're scared, Primrose," Janitor Gary said. "I'm scared too! But the children want to help. We have to at least let them *try!*"

Coach Johnson licked her lips. "It's too late," she said. "The compass is still missing! Destroying the chest is our only option!" She reached for the axe again, her eyes darkening with determination. "Step back and watch, children! It's all in the glutes!"

Harvey swallowed, gathering his courage.

Sometimes, being brave doesn't mean scaling a mountain peak, or jumping out of a plane, or facing down a hungry wombat.

Sometimes, being brave just means telling the truth.

Coach Johnson raised the axe above her head, preparing to swing.

"Wait!" Harvey shouted in panic. *It's me! I took the compass!*

Harvey's Confession

"It's me," Harvey said again, his voice thick with shame. "*I'm* the reason the curse is back. This is all my fault."

Harvey reached into his pocket and pulled out the compass. For something that had weighed so heavily in his pocket, it felt surprisingly light in his hand. "I took this from the lost-and-found box," he said, showing it to the others. "It reminded me of the compass my grandfather used to use when he went on his adventures. I thought . . . I thought . . ."

"Speak up, boy!" Coach Johnson barked, the axe

suspended mid-swing above her head. "You thought *what*?"

Harvey's cheeks were flaming with embarrassment. Beneath his T-shirt, even the tips of his wings had turned pink.

(Yes. For the last time, *Harvey had wings.*)

"I thought . . . maybe it was meant for me," he admitted. "That finding the compass meant I really *was* supposed to follow in my grandfather's footsteps after all." He looked down, clutching the compass a little tighter in his fingers. "It sounds silly, but I thought it was a *sign.*"

"Of course it doesn't sound silly," Stella said firmly. "It doesn't sound silly *at all.*"

"*Everyone* makes mistakes," Nevaeh added. "One time, during a rocket launch at NASA, I forgot to account for the change in momentum due to decreased mass and fluctuating velocity." She shook her head at the memory. "I mean, I was only eight years old at the time, but still."

Coach Johnson was still holding the enormous axe above her head. Her muscular arms were beginning to quiver with effort, beads of sweat rolling down her chin.

Harvey felt a wave of emotion wash through him. "I never meant to cause any trouble," he said. "I thought I could return it before anyone found out. But there were always so many people around, and then the box disappeared, and . . ." He trailed off, shaking his head. "Everything just got out of hand. I mean, there's a *kraken* loose in the school. A *kraken*! And it's all my fault! How could I be so *selfish*?"

"Hey," Stella said firmly. "Watch it. That's my *friend* you're talking about, you know."

Harvey looked down at the old-fashioned camera around his neck. "I just wanted to make my grandfather proud. He's the one who gave me this camera, you know? He used to talk about all the trips we'd take together when I was older. All the places we'd photograph: the northern lights in

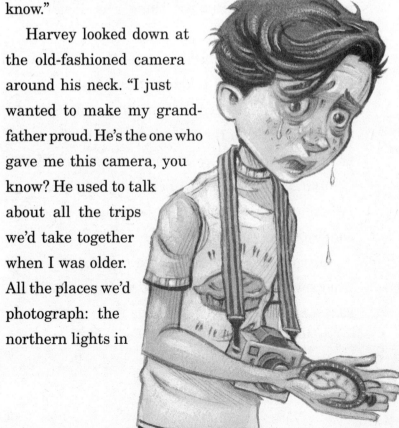

Iceland, the great pyramids of South America, the vast lentil fields of Middle Saskatchewan . . ."

"They really *are* magnificent," Nevaeh murmured knowledgeably. "Lentils as far as the eye can see."

Coach Johnson was *still* holding the axe above her head, the veins in her powerful neck throbbing with effort.

Harvey paused, shaking his head. "It's funny," he said. "He was always talking about all the places we'd *go* together. But the thing was, I just liked *being* with him. It didn't matter where." He gave a small shiver, remembering one of the photographs his grandfather had taken at his camp during his summit of Mount Everest: a tiny, windswept tent clinging grimly to the frozen rock face. His grandfather had loved it; to Harvey, it had looked like a nightmare. "Although, *preferably,* I'd prefer to be somewhere with heat," he added. "And air-conditioning. And Wi-Fi. And—"

An ominous shriek echoed up the stairwell from several floors below, cutting Harvey off mid-sentence.

Stella looked at Nevaeh.

Nevaeh looked at Harvey.

Harvey looked at Stella.

Janitor Gary looked at Coach Johnson.

Coach Johnson looked up at her axe. It was wobbling unsteadily above her head.

"Look," Nevaeh said. "I'm not saying I definitely *believe* in the curse, but maybe we should . . . put the compass back? Just to be on the safe side?"

Harvey swallowed. "Yeah," he said. "That might be a good idea."

But as he stepped toward the lost-and-found box, Stella reached out, grabbing his arm.

"Wait," she said. "Not yet."

Harvey paused, his stomach fluttering with dread. "Why not?"

"Because," Stella said, holding up the treasure map for him to see, "something tells me we might need a compass."

29

The Basement

"Are you sure we shouldn't have asked Coach Johnson and Janitor Gary to come along?" Harvey asked, shoving his end of the lost-and-found box down another step. "I mean, they *are* adults. Plus, they're the only ones who know where we're going!"

"Please. You *saw* Coach Johnson drop the axe on her foot," Stella reminded him, pausing to wipe the sweat from her brow. When she pulled her hand away, her forehead was streaked with dirt; as well as being cursed, the lost-and-found box was also *extremely* dusty. "Besides, she and Janitor Gary need time to catch up. They haven't seen each other in fifty years!"

"Technically, they've seen each other every day," Nevaeh pointed out. "They've just been *ignoring* each other for fifty years. Harvey, can you lift your end a little higher? We don't want the box to tip over."

"You know, this would go a lot faster if

you helped carry it too," Harvey pointed out, grunting with effort. "This thing is *heavy*."

Nevaeh looked down at her clothes. Despite everything they'd been through, her outfit was still spotless white. "Don't be silly," she told Harvey. "It's *picture day*."

Stella rolled her eyes.

Panting heavily, she and Harvey managed to carry the wooden chest the rest of the way down the

stairs and lower it heavily to the floor in front of the basement door.

The sign on the door read STRANGEVILLE SCHOOL BASEMENT: ABSOLUTELY DO NOT ENTER UNDER ANY CIRCUMSTANCES. SERIOUSLY! THIS MEANS YOU!

"Oh, right," Harvey said weakly. "I forgot about that."

Stella patted his arm encouragingly. "Everything's going to be fine," she said. "Well, *probably,* anyway."

Nevaeh peered down at the map. "According to Janitor Gary and Coach Johnson, we take a left, another left, two rights, three lefts, another right, six lefts, and then, finally, a U-turn."

"Well, that sounds easy enough," Stella said.

"Yeah," Harvey said. "I think we might have different opinions on what the word 'easy' means."

"We just need to follow the directions," Nevaeh said, her voice firm. "After all, how big can the basement be?" she asked, pushing open the door in front of them.

The basement was huge.

In fact, it was enormous.

In fact, it was unbelievably, *inconceivably* vast.

The children stared incredulously into the cavernous depths before them: an echoing ocean of space that seemed to stretch forever in every direction.

The room was dimly lit, with the dull clank of machinery filling the air and puddles of oil skimming the floor at regular intervals.

It smelled like rat droppings and despair.

Nevaeh straightened her shoulders. "Come on," she said, leading them into the basement. "This way."

Harvey and Stella exchanged a glance.

Then, after picking up the treasure chest, they followed Nevaeh into the darkness.

The basement twisted and turned in strange, confusing ways. The ceiling above them was lined with pipes hissing steam at irregular intervals.

The room seemed to get bigger with every step.

Harvey could hear something dripping nearby. He hoped it was a pipe.

"Follow me," Nevaeh called, ducking low beneath a half-fallen metal beam. "I think it's this way!"

Their arms aching from the effort of carrying the box, Harvey and Stella ducked after her. The narrow corridors were like a maze, leading them one way, then another, deeper and deeper into the basement.

Harvey wasn't sure, but it felt as though the floor was beginning to slant downward, leading them lower and lower into the bowels of the school. The overhead lights were growing further and further apart, the darkness creeping up on them from every side.

In the distance, he heard a wolf howl.

A-ooooooooo!

Nevaeh squinted down at the map, struggling to see in the light of a single overhead bulb. "Wolves," she said. "We must be getting close."

Another howl echoed through the air, closer this time.

Harvey was trying to remember what to do if

they encountered a wolf in person. He was pretty sure you were supposed to run as quickly as you could in the opposite direction.

Harvey was, of course, completely wrong.

If you encounter a wolf in person, you should under *no* circumstances run as quickly as you can in the opposite direction.

Instead, you should stand tall and make yourself look as large as possible. Calmly but slowly, back away while maintaining eye contact.

If the wolf doesn't retreat and is acting aggressively by holding its tail high, raising its hackles, barking, or howling, you should yell and throw things at it while continuing to back away.

Acceptable phrases to yell include "Scram!," "Get out of here!," and "Your mother was a hamster and your father smelt of elderberries!"

But, anyway.

Enough about wolf attacks!

Let's get back to Harvey.

He was just taking another step when the lights abruptly winked out, plunging the trio into complete and total darkness.

The Basement, Continued

Harvey sighed.

"Of *course* the lights went out," he said. "Why *wouldn't* they?"

Another wolf howl sounded, eerily close to their heels.

After dropping his end of the chest, Harvey fumbled for the old-fashioned camera around his neck and twisted the cap off the lens. He raised the camera in front of him, flicked the Speedlite into the on position, and snapped a picture.

The flash went off, briefly illuminating the basement in bright white light.

Harvey shrieked as a face jumped out of the darkness in front of him, just inches from his own. *"Ghost!"*

In the darkness, Stella rolled her eyes. "It's me," she said. "I've literally been standing next to you the entire time, remember?"

"Are you sure?" Harvey asked. He took another picture, illuminating the flash once more.

Nevaeh held her hands up, shielding her eyes from the glare. "Would you stop that?" she asked. "You're hurting my eyes!"

"Sorry," Harvey said, lowering his camera. "I just . . . don't like the dark."

"The only thing we have to fear is our own imagination," Nevaeh said. "Well, that and wolves, I suppose."

Stella swung her backpack from her shoulder and unzipped the main compartment. There was a momentary shuffling noise, and then a sharp crack.

A second later, a pool of light spread around them, pushing back the darkness.

Harvey blinked in the sudden light. "Is that a

glow stick?" he asked. "Do you just carry *glow sticks* around with you?"

"What?" Stella asked. "You don't?"

She handed another glow stick to Nevaeh, then passed one to Harvey, and waited while they cracked them to life.

Nevaeh swept the glow stick over the treasure map, a flicker of doubt passing over her face.

"Oh no," Harvey said. "Don't tell me we're lost."

"Of course we're not *lost*," Nevaeh said. "We're just . . . temporarily misplaced."

"'Temporarily misplaced'?" Stella repeated. "What is *that* supposed to mean?"

"It means I know we're somewhere around *here*," Nevaeh said, gesturing to one corner of the map. "I'm just not exactly sure *where*."

Stella turned to Harvey, bouncing a little in excitement. "Harvey!" she said. "This is it!"

Harvey's stomach gave a nervous flip. "Uh-uh," he said. "No way. Definitely not."

Stella spread her arms wide. "You heard Nevaeh! We're *lost*!"

"Temporarily misplaced," Nevaeh corrected her.

"We're going to be *permanently* misplaced if we can't find our way out of here," Stella said. "Come on, Harvey. *This* is the reason you found the compass! You can be a hero! *You can end the curse!*"

Harvey blinked.

"But . . . um . . . aren't I the one who *started* the curse?" he asked. "I mean, when I took the compass from the lost-and-found box in the first place?"

"Details," Stella said airily, waving off his objection. "This is your moment! This is your *destiny*!"

Harvey took a deep breath.

Maybe Stella was right.

Maybe he *wasn't* supposed to follow in his grandfather's footsteps. Maybe he was supposed to make his *own* path.

Maybe he really *could* save Strangeville!

"Okay," Harvey said aloud, reaching for the compass.

He could do this.

He *wanted* to do this.

He *had* to do this.

Harvey was going to do this.

"Right," he said, peering down at the compass. "First things first: Does anyone know what the little letters on the sides mean?"

The Pirate Ship

Twenty minutes later, the children were somehow even *more* lost than before.

"I don't understand," Harvey said, spinning in a slow circle. "Are we sure the *N* stands for 'north'? The needle keeps spinning around!"

On his shoulder, Percy nipped at his ear.

"Compasses point to the *magnetic* North Pole, not the *geographic* North Pole," Nevaeh said. "If Strangeville is located on one of the agonic lines that combine both poles, it could account for fluctuations in the needle."

"Yeah," Stella said. "Or maybe we're just cursed."

Percy gave another nip, harder this time.

"We're running out of time," Harvey said fretfully. "Nevaeh, let me see the map again. There's got to be some way to—Percy, would you *stop that?*"

Percy gave Harvey's ear a final, painful tug and launched himself into the air. As the children watched, the parrot spread his wings and flapped confidently down the corridor and into the darkness.

"Percy!" Harvey shouted, shoving the treasure map into his back pocket as he chased after the errant parrot. "Wait!"

Nevaeh and Stella looked at each other. Then, grabbing the chest between them, they followed.

Percy led the children through the maze of twisting hallways, Harvey catching occasional glimpses of the parrot's bright red-and-yellow feathers in the dim light of his glow stick.

Even in the darkness, the parrot seemed to know exactly where he was going. Harvey followed as best he could, tripping his way over exposed pipes and struggling to keep up with his feathery friend.

At last, Percy slowed down and looped several times overhead before fluttering back down to Harvey's shoulder.

"*There* you are," Harvey said, scolding the parrot. "I was worried! You can't just . . ."

Harvey's voice trailed off as he caught sight of the room in front of them, bathed in a soft greenish glow.

It was implausible.

It was improbable.

It was practically *impossible*.

And yet, there it was: a shipwreck.

The enormous wooden hull of the ship was tilted to one side, its timber frame grown warped and skeletal over the years. Dust lay heavy underfoot, and thick coils of rotting rope were looped here and there. A snarling sea serpent was carved into the prow of the ship, wings unfurled, its teeth bared in warning.

There was no way to tell how long the wreck had been there. A faint greenish glow seemed to cling to the ship, pulsing eerily in the darkness.

Harvey felt as though they had stumbled upon

something private, a lonely grave site that was never meant to be found.

"Whoa," Stella breathed. "It's actually *real.*"

"This is impossible," Nevaeh said, shaking her head. "We must be hallucinating. You know, now that I think about it, the fish fingers *did* taste extra fishy today."

"I wonder who the ship belonged to," Harvey said, staring at the dusty wreckage. "Probably someone with a really cool name, like Captain Dreadbeard. Or . . . Egbert the Horrible!"

Stella crossed her arms in front of her chest. "What makes you think it was a man?" she asked coolly. "You know, women pirates were a lot more common than you'd think."

Stella was right.

While pirating was predominantly a male occupation, many women pirates existed throughout history, including but not limited to Anne Bonny, Mary Read, Teuta of Illyria, Charlotte de Berry, and the colorfully named Sadie the Goat, who was known for headbutting her victims.

One of the most successful pirates in history

was a woman named Ching Shih, who at one point commanded over eighteen hundred sailing ships and crew numbering sixty thousand. While most pirates were eventually caught and executed for their crimes, Ching Shih was able to retire with both her life *and* her ill-gotten loot and lived happily to the age of sixty-nine.

Which, back in the day, was very, *very* old.

But, anyway.

Enough about pirates!

Let's get back to Harvey.

"So . . . what do we do now?" he asked nervously.

"Come on," Stella said, nodding toward the wreckage of the pirate ship. "Let's get the chest inside."

Harvey and Stella followed Nevaeh onto the ship, climbing over the remains of the railing. The floor beneath them was warped with age, making Harvey's sensitive stomach pitch and roll with every step.

Once aboard, he and Stella lowered the chest carefully to the floor. As Nevaeh opened the top, Harvey reached into his pocket and pulled the compass free.

He took a deep breath.

"Well," he said aloud, holding the dented brass compass above the open chest, "here goes noth—"

A pirate cutlass whooshed through the air, cutting Harvey off mid-word.

Captain Buttertoes

The sword *thwock*ed into the wooden post behind them, its blade nearly grazing the side of Nevaeh's head. At the top of the ship's crow's nest, a mysterious figure stood silhouetted in the darkness.

"Hey, *watch it!*" Nevaeh said sharply, reaching up to check her hair. "It's *picture day,* you know!"

The mysterious figure jumped from the crow's nest and slid down the rigging to land with a flourish in front of the children.

He was, quite obviously, a pirate.

His well-worn frock coat billowed past his knees; his dark, curly hair fell nearly to his shoulders. He looked startlingly like the well-known singer-songwriter Alfred "Weird Al" Yankovic.

(If Harvey had known who Weird Al was, he would have been impressed by the resemblance.)

Nevaeh clapped politely. "Impressive costume," she said. "Very authentic!"

Ignoring her, the pirate reached out to pluck the cutlass from the wooden post. He brandished it menacingly in the children's direction.

Up close, the sword looked very authentic indeed.

"Arrr," the pirate snarled. "And just what do you think ye be doing with Captain Buttertoes's treasure chest?"

There was a moment of silence.

"I'm sorry," Harvey ventured at last. "Did you say your name was Captain *Buttertoes?*"

"Aye," the pirate said, a touch of defensiveness in his voice. " 'Tis a long story."

Stella tilted her head to the side. "Did you step in butter or something?" she asked.

"Enough chitchat!" Captain Buttertoes snapped, neatly sidestepping the question. "You're here to steal me treasure chest, aren't ye! *Be honest!*"

"No!" Harvey said, nervously eyeing the pirate's sword. "I swear! We're actually here to *return* the chest!"

"Oho!" said Captain Buttertoes, switching gears. "I see how it is! So, me treasure isn't *good* enough for you, eh?"

"What?" Harvey asked in confusion. "No!"

"Not all pirates are obsessed with gold, ye know!" Captain Buttertoes said indignantly. "Some of us appreciate the simpler things in life! Sure, she might not be stuffed with treasure," he went on, nodding toward the open chest at their feet. "But you'll always find what you're looking for in her depths! 'Tis magic, it is!"

"Wait," Harvey said. "So, it really *is* a lost-and-found box after all?"

"But the chest doesn't work," Stella told the pirate, shaking her head. "Things come back *different*. Things come back *wrong*!"

"Aye, and so what if they do?" Captain Buttertoes asked. "Do ye know how hard it is to find an enchanted chest?" he demanded. "You can't expect it to be perf . . ."

The pirate trailed off, his expression suddenly sharpening as he caught sight of the compass clutched in Harvey's hand.

"Arrr," he growled, jabbing his cutlass in Harvey's direction. "Is that what I think it is?"

Harvey gulped.

Nevaeh leaned forward, examining the sword more closely. "It really *does* look quite authentic," she said. "Although, historically speaking, the blade should be *slightly* thinner."

"I swear, it's not what it looks like," Harvey said quickly, as Stella tugged Nevaeh away from the sword. "I mean, it *is* what it looks like, but not really. I didn't realize the compass belonged to anyone! It was a mistake!"

Captain Buttertoes shook his head mournfully.

"So, you've stolen from the chest, have ye?" he asked. "I'm afraid Fluffy won't be liking that. . . ."

Harvey and Stella exchanged worried glances.

"Fluffy?" Harvey asked nervously. "Who's Fluffy?"

Captain Buttertoes smiled a *deeply* unpleasant smile.

"Would you like to meet her?" he asked.

Pursing his salt-weathered lips, the pirate uttered a long, low whistle.

"Here, Fluffy!" he called. "Time for lunch!"

Fluffy

The basement gave an ominous lurch as the ceiling rippled overhead, clouds of dust and bits of plaster raining down on their heads. The kraken swam easily through the ocean of concrete, its powerful tentacles ripping the path clear.

The children shrieked as several of Fluffy's enormous, slimy tentacles burst through the ceiling, waving menacingly in front of them. The huge, sucker-covered tentacles smelled of rotting fish and whale blubber.

"Easy, girl, easy," Captain Buttertoes said soothingly. "I know you're hungry. 'Tis soon enough you'll be having a warm meal in your belly."

Harvey gave Stella and Nevaeh a wide-eyed look, his voice pitching upward in alarm. "Is he talking about *us*? Are *we* the warm meal?"

Nevaeh shrieked again, ducking low to avoid a tentacle that swept past her head.

Stella dodged to the side, narrowly avoiding yet *another* of Fluffy's horrible, grasping tentacles. "The compass," she yelled. "Put the compass *back!*"

Harvey nodded.

His hands were trembling, his fingers slick with sweat.

Still, as he looked down at the compass in his hand, he couldn't help the rush of memories that washed over him: The scent of lemon furniture polish clinging to his grandfather's desk. The squeak of the wooden globe as his grandfather turned it, pointing down at the continents with sure fingers. The excitement in his grandfather's voice as he planned one adventure after another—trips they would never take, now.

Harvey had spent his entire life trying to live up to his grandfather's reputation, trying to prove that he had what it took to follow in his grandfather's enormous footprints.

But Harvey needed to face the truth.

He didn't like heights, or heat, or sand.

He didn't like mountains, or jungles, or deserts.

He didn't like *adventure*.

And that was fine.

Harvey was brave.

He was loyal.

He was honest.

He was really, *really* good at jumping jacks.

And he was about to save his school from a mythical sea beast.

Even with a lifetime of adventure beneath his belt, Harvey doubted if his grandfather had ever been able to say *that*.

Harvey took a deep breath, squeezing his eyes shut tight.

Then, finally letting go of his expectations, he tossed the compass back into the chest.

Nothing happened.

Harvey opened one eye and peered down at the lost-and-found box. The eerie green glow continued to pour from the top of the chest, pulsing and

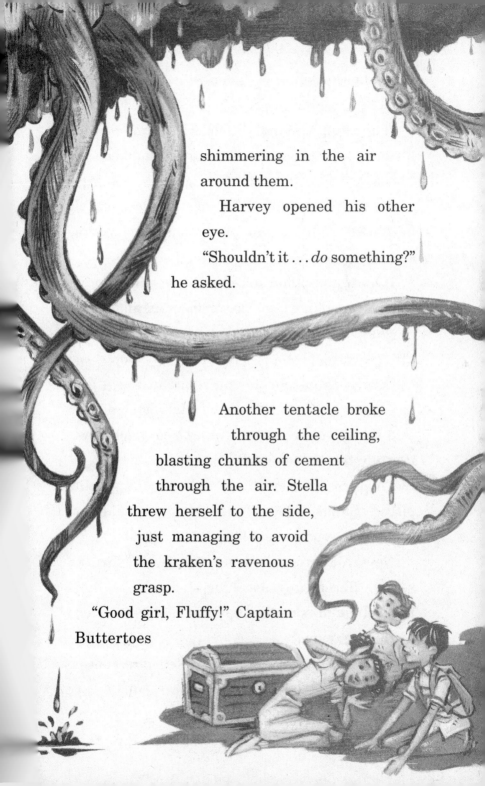

shimmering in the air around them.

Harvey opened his other eye.

"Shouldn't it . . . *do* something?" he asked.

Another tentacle broke through the ceiling, blasting chunks of cement through the air. Stella threw herself to the side, just managing to avoid the kraken's ravenous grasp.

"Good girl, Fluffy!" Captain Buttertoes

called encouragingly. "Avenge me stolen treasure!"

"I don't understand!" Stella cried, jumping nimbly over a pile of rubble. "The curse should be *over*! The stolen treasure was *returned*!"

On the other side of the chest, Nevaeh visibly hesitated. "Well," she admitted, "maybe not *all* the stolen treasure."

Harvey and Stella stared at Nevaeh in surprise, Fluffy's forbidding tentacles momentarily forgotten.

"Wait a second," Stella said. "*You* stole something from the lost-and-found box?"

"But . . . you said the entire premise of a lost-and-found box was ridiculous," Harvey said. "You said that if you're properly organized, you'll never lose anything to begin with."

"'A place for everything, and everything in its place,'" Stella added. "That's what you said. You said it was your personal motto!"

Nevaeh cleared her throat. "Yes, well," she said stiffly. "Technically speaking, I didn't *lose* anything; I *found* something. It just happened to . . . not belong to me."

"Thar she blows!" Percy squawked, interrupting the children.

In all the excitement, they had completely forgotten about him.

The parrot hopped back and forth from one foot to another, bobbing its brightly feathered head toward the kraken in warning. *"Thar she blows!"*

The children had just enough time to throw themselves to the deck as Fluffy swept another massive tentacle through the air, missing them by mere inches.

"Arrr, ye bilious birdbrain!" Captain Buttertoes said, grabbing wildly for the parrot. "Whose side are you on, anyway?"

Percy fluttered quickly out of the pirate's reach and landed safely on Harvey's shoulder instead.

Harvey felt a rush of affection toward the small parrot.

"Nice work, Percy," he said, reaching up to give the bird a pat.

Percy bit him.

The giant kraken was growing frustrated now, whipping its arms through the air with frenzied hunger. Again and again Fluffy lashed out, swiping at the children with goo-coated tentacles.

"She can't reach us!" Harvey called. "Stay on the floor!"

The ceiling gave an ominous creak, straining under the weight of the massive monster.

"It's not going to hold much longer!" Stella cried.

"Nevaeh, whatever you took, you have to put it back!" Harvey said urgently.

Nevaeh nodded.

She reached awkwardly into her pocket and managed to wriggle out something small and fuzzy-looking, hand-knit from delicate pink yarn.

It appeared to be a tiny little hat.

Captain Buttertoes gave an outraged cry. "So, ye've stolen Fluffy's baby bonnet as well! Have ye no shame, you lily-livered landlubbers?"

"I thought it could be a wombat hat," Nevaeh said. "For Bunsen. Bunsen Burner," she clarified. "My rescue wombat. Sometimes he gets cold at night!" she added defensively. "Wombats can have trouble regulating their body temperature, you know!"

"Huh," Harvey said, staring down at the hat. "I did *not* see that coming."

(I *told* you that wombats would be important!)

The ceiling gave another *creeeaaakkk,* shuddering beneath Fluffy's weight.

"I'm sorry!" Nevaeh said. "How was I supposed to know the curse was real?"

"Aha!" Stella said. "So, you *admit* it's real!"

A drop of goo fell from one of Fluffy's tentacles, splatting wetly onto Harvey's cheek. "Um, people?" he asked, a touch of hysteria in his voice. *"Could we maybe argue about it later?"*

"Harvey's right," Stella said. "Put the hat back, quick!"

Nevaeh nodded again. Ducking low beneath Fluffy's questing tentacles, she crawled forward on her elbows.

"Don't worry, Bunsen," she whispered. "I'll buy you a hat!"

"All hands on deck!" Captain Buttertoes bellowed. "Attack, Fluffy! *Attack!*"

But it was too late.

With a quick flick of her wrist, Nevaeh flung the hat back into the treasure chest.

It was done.

What Happened Next

The strange, greenish glow that spilled from the top of the treasure chest grew suddenly brighter, filling the basement with a harsh, unnatural light.

The children turned away, shielding their eyes from the glow. A fierce wind kicked up out of nowhere: an odd, almost *salty* breeze that swirled and plunged all around them. Harvey could feel it tugging at his clothes and whipping at his hair; the treasure map was ripped from his back pocket and fluttered out of reach. "Abandon ship, Fluffy!" Captain Buttertoes shouted, staggering against the gale. His frock coat billowed out behind him as the wind buffeted the pirate forward, toward the chest. *"We're going down!"*

The light was growing brighter and brighter, an unbearable, incandescent shade of green.

"Hold on!" Stella yelled, grabbing at Harvey's hand. "And keep your eyes shut!" She reached for Nevaeh's hand as well, and the three friends clung tightly to one another as the wind howled angrily past.

Even through his tightly closed eyelids, the eerie green light was bright enough to hurt Harvey's eyes. He clutched Percy to his chest, sheltering him from the storm as best he could.

All around them, the basement seemed to shudder. Fluffy's enormous tentacles wreaked havoc as the kraken was sucked into the vortex of the lost-and-found box, returning from whence she'd come.

"We'll be back!" Captain Buttertoes vowed, his voice just barely audible above the howling shriek of the wind. *"We'll be back!"*

The heavy wooden lid of the treasure chest slammed shut with a decisive crack.

For a second, the children remained huddled together, their eyes squeezed shut and their hands clenched tightly in one another's.

And then Stella opened her eyes to peer cautiously around the basement.

"They're gone," she said. "We did it!"

"We did it?" Harvey repeated, opening his eyes in surprise. He looked around the basement, realization dawning. "We *did* it!"

And, before he could think, he launched himself forward and enveloped Nevaeh and Stella in an enormous hug.

Nevaeh pulled away, glancing down at her outfit in horror.

Harvey winced. Nevaeh's previously pristine white shirt and skirt were now streaked gray with dirt and bore the faint marks of shrimp-flavored Jell-O, flecks of dried red paint, and the unmistakable smear of bird poop.

Yes, bird poop.

Percy was still working on his manners.

"Er . . . sorry about that," Harvey said. He shifted awkwardly from one foot to the other as Nevaeh peered down at her ruined clothes. "Maybe there's a dry cleaner nearby or something?"

To his surprise, Nevaeh laughed. "Who cares?" she asked. *"We did it!"* And she launched herself forward and crushed Harvey and Stella into another massive hug.

Who knows how long the children would have stayed there, hugging each other in triumph, if Percy hadn't poked his head up to peer alertly around the basement.

"Uh-oh," the parrot squawked. "Ye be doomed again!"

Certain Doom?

"**P**ercy is right," Stella said, peering around the basement in dismay. "I mean, *look* at this place. How are we supposed to get out of here?"

Fluffy's lethal tentacles had done more damage than they'd realized. Massive piles of rubble were strewn about the basement; the floor was now littered with sharp-edged metal pipes and broken pieces of machinery. Entire walls were missing in places, and both the floor and the ceiling had gaping holes.

Harvey edged away from a particularly lethal-looking length of jagged pipe, hoping his tetanus shot was up to date.

Miraculously, the wreck of the pirate ship was still standing, having protected the children from the worst of the kraken's rampage.

"What about your wings?" Nevaeh asked Harvey. "Can you fly out and get help?"

Harvey shook his head. "The ceiling is too low," he said. "Plus, even if I *could,* I have no idea where I'm going."

Stella sighed. "Even if we still *had* the treasure map, it would be useless now," she said, gesturing around the ruins of the basement. "We're *stuck.*"

"Maybe not," Nevaeh said, picking her way over the railing and toward a nearby pile of wreckage. "Look!" Half-buried beneath a crumbled pile of concrete stood a large, blocky piece of machinery, roughly the size and shape of a chest freezer.

Harvey squinted at it in confusion. "It looks like an ice machine," he said. "How is an *ice machine* going to help us?"

"It's not an ice machine," Nevaeh said impatiently. "It's a backup generator! The same one

Janitor Gary and Coach Johnson must have found, all those years ago! If we can get it up and running, I can tap into the school's power grid and trace the electrical wiring back to the first floor using a makeshift voltage detector!"

Harvey blinked.

"Er . . . ," he said. "We can do *what*, now?"

"Just trust me," Nevaeh told him. "I'm a rocket scientist!"

With quick, sure movements, she pulled open the generator's side panel and rummaged knowledgeably around inside.

After a moment, her face fell.

"The battery's dead," she said, looking up at Harvey and Stella. "It's *hopeless*. In order to get the generator running, we'd need a parallel connection–capable 100Ah lithium-iron-phosphate deep-cycle battery."

Stella raised her eyebrows.

As Harvey and Nevaeh watched, she swung her backpack from her shoulder and unzipped the top.

Harvey shook his head. "Oh, *come on*," he said. "There's no way you have one of *those* in your . . ."

He trailed off as Stella pulled a truly enormous battery free from her backpack, staggering slightly beneath its weight.

To be fair, it was twenty-six pounds.

"Here you go," Stella told Nevaeh, passing it over. "One parallel connection–capable 100Ah lithium-iron-phosphate deep-cycle battery at your service!"

Harvey stared at her in disbelief. "Seriously?"

"What?" Stella asked, shrugging. "You never know when a good battery is going to come in handy."

Nevaeh pulled the old battery free and slotted the new one into the generator. After quickly connecting the wires, she flipped the power on.

A loud buzz filled the air as the generator rumbled to life, the lights blinking on overhead. Loosened by the machinery's vibrations, bits of the remaining ceiling began to plummet. A large crack appeared in the floor beneath the pirate ship and began to widen rapidly.

"Come on," Stella said, narrowly dodging a chunk of falling concrete. "Let's get out of here before this whole place collapses!"

Nevaeh was carefully testing each wire, tracing the path of the electrical current. "Got it!" she said, her voice sure. "Follow me!"

Harvey hesitated, turning to peer back at the now innocent-looking treasure chest. "But what about the lost-and-found box?" he asked. "What if it reappears? The curse could start all over again!"

Stella grabbed his hand, pulling him forward. "Don't worry about the treasure chest!" she called over her shoulder. "This whole place is about to go under!"

With Percy still clinging tightly to his shoulder, Harvey allowed Stella to tug him along behind her. He cast one last glance in the direction of the pirate ship.

The ship was sinking, being swallowed up by the ever-widening crack in the basement floor. Harvey caught a final glimpse of the wooden treasure chest as it disappeared from view, buried beneath an ocean of crumbling concrete.

For just a moment, the box seemed to *glow*.

Harvey turned away.

And this time he didn't look back.

Picture Day

"Now, don't forget," the photographer said, bending low in front of the camera. "On the count of three, everyone say, 'Strange-ville!'"

The children had managed to find their way back to the surface at last—hungrier, thirstier, and certainly *dirtier* than they had ever been in their lives.

To Harvey's surprise, Nevaeh had insisted on having their photograph taken together before the final bell rang.

"After all," she told Harvey, shaking the worst

of the concrete dust from her hair, "it *is* picture day."

"One!" the photographer called.

Stella looped her arm around Nevaeh's shoulders, pulling her close.

"I've been thinking," Nevaeh said. "A carbon monoxide leak *would* explain everything that happened in the basement. Auditory and visual hallucinations, an unexplained feeling of dread, the explosion leading up to the structural collapse . . ."

Stella rolled her eyes. "For the last time," she said, "curses are real. *Deal with it.*"

"Two!" the photographer called.

On Stella's other side, Harvey smiled, leaning into the shot.

Maybe *he* would become a school-picture photographer when he grew older.

That had to be a nice, safe profession, didn't it?

Didn't it?

"Three!" the photographer called.

"Strangeville!" the children shouted in unison, grinning for all they were worth.

Percy fluttered in alarm.

And, leaning forward, he bit Harvey's ear.

An Announcement

Good afternoon, Strangeville. This is Vice Principal Capozzi here with your final update for the day!

I'm pleased to announce that the *small* issue of our cursed lost-and-found box has now been re-solved, and the kraken has returned to its watery depths!

So long, terrifying sea beast!

Safe travels!

Janitor Gary, who is currently in the process of draining the West Hallway, informs me that all sharks *will*, of course, be rehomed to loving families. Mean-while, any students suffering from shark bites and/or other minor injuries should report to the nurse's office, where Nurse Porter informs me that "leeches will be available on a first come, first served" basis.

Ha-ha! What a wonderful sense of humor Nurse Porter has!

Moving on, the French and German clubs would like to announce that all remaining bake-sale items are currently half-price! All half-price items *are* final sale. I repeat, there are *no returns* on any items, including those covered in kraken slime.

Mmm, mmm.

Kraken slime!

As picture day draws to a close at Strangeville, I'd like to remind all students that photographs *must* be taken individually. Again, group photos are *not* allowed! On a related note, parrots are also *strictly* forbidden. I cannot stress this enough, people: *no parrots will be allowed in your class photographs.*

Ahem.

Yes.

Finally, I'm excited to announce that a new substitute teacher will be arriving at Strangeville School next week! I'm told she comes with excellent references and is, most assuredly, *not* evil!

I repeat, our new substitute teacher is positively, undeniably, most *certainly* not evil!

That's all for now, Strangeville!

Have a wonderful evening!

And remember:

Be kind. Be safe. Be curious. But most of all . . . be afraid.

Acknowledgments

I'm so grateful to everyone at Random House for the making of this book, including Caroline Abbey, Jasmine Hodge, and Michelle Nagler. Carrie Hannigan, Ellen Goff, and everyone at HG Literary, thanks so much for always being there for me. Karen Sherman and Barbara Bakowski, thank you for catching my (many) mistakes. Thanks to Jen Valero, April Ward, and Brett Helquist for this unbelievably awesome cover. Fitz, thank you for giving me so many great ideas! Wyle, thanks for telling me when my ideas are terrible. And finally, Ben, thank you for everything, always. You're the best.